THE

MW01127754

SPECTACULAR
TALES II

Another thrilling anthology of short stories by some of the rising stars in independent publishing. In this second collection of short Speculative Fiction we bring you another treasure chest of great Science Fiction and Fantasy. Here you will find stories of intergalactic policemen, virtual soldiers, spirited princesses, lonesome spacemen and even megalomaniac dogs and kleptomaniac goats.

So dust off your old suit of armour and grab your blaster pistol and come join us in exploring more 'Spectacular Tales'.

ISBN-13: 978-1518629068
ISBN-10: 1518629067

EDITED BY CHRIS P. RAVEN AND DANI J CAILE
COVER ART BY BOOK BIRDY DESIGNS

THE INDIE COLLABORATION GREW OUT OF A GROUP
OF INDEPENDENT AUTHORS WHO DECIDED TO SHOW
THE WORLD HOW GREAT WORKS OF FICTION CAN BE,
WITHOUT THE INVOLVEMENT OF ANY LARGE
PUBLISHING COMPANIES, BY CREATING A DIRECT
CHANNEL BETWEEN THEMSELVES AND THEIR
READERS. EACH AUTHOR IN THIS ANTHOLOGY HAS
FREELY DONATED THEIR TIME AND WORK AND ARE
COMMITTED TO THE INDIE COLLABORATION'S CAUSE:

"WE OFFER THE BEST OF INDIE WRITING IN BITE SIZE
PIECES AND WHEREVER POSSIBLE, FOR FREE."

WE HOPE YOU ENJOY OUR BOOKS.
IF YOU DID, THEN PLEASE LEAVE A REVIEW WHERE
YOU PURCHASED IT.

READ ORDER

41
107 (6)
53
89 (10)

15 (12)   27 (14)   125

(5·45·99·141)
(63- 113)

CONTENTS

Chaos on Cass
By Chris Raven

Part One: Arrival
Cass III (The Third Planet of the Eta Cassiopeiae System, 20LY from Sol and held in fealty to the Terran Star Empire by the Imperial House of Lein Rocha)

The Interrogator

Machinegun fire ricochets above my head. I'm pinned down behind this low brick wall. It borders an old Earth oak tree of all things. I guess it's an oak, only ever seen them in vids. The would-be assassins are using slug throwers. Slug throwers! Real archaic trajectory weapons, how quaint. Better not underestimate them though, my laser pistol has the advantage of range and accuracy but I still need to aim. The three masked assassins across the street? All they have to do is keep the lead coming and besides, slugs are just so damned messy.

"Bloody terrorists again, eh Jorich?" I look into my partner's dark green eyes, they stare lifelessly back up at me. Dead at last the poor Bastard.

Eight hours earlier

Captain Harford Beydo watched with barely hidden contempt as the shuttle touched down on the spaceport's blast scarred landing strip. Lieutenant Vasco Higani stood silently beside him in the first class observation lounge and knew better than to comment, especially when the Captain was in one of his moods. Beydo had been chief of police on Eta Cassiopeiae for the past three years, when the rich garden world had been granted to House Lien Rocha by Emperor Lexomede A'juan on Terra. House Orenstein, who had previously held the system and its lucrative third planet, had temporarily fallen from grace and losing the food production contract on Cass III had been old Oberon Orenstein's punishment.

Standard procedure dictated that all key administrative posts were filled by Lein Rochan representatives of Executive or Nobel class and Beydo had arrived from Alpha Centari IV, the Lein Rochan homeworld, to replace the outgoing Orenstein Chief of Police. Higani, a native Cassian and graduate of the Imperial Guild of Psions, had been allowed to stay on in his post of lieutenant. He had come to know Beydo quite well over the past three years and had found him to be an effective, if temperamental leader, strict but thankfully able to prioritize law enforcement over politics, something his predecessor had not been able to do.

Higani could feel the frustration and anger radiating from his superior's psyche. The Captain had always been an open book to Higani, despite his attempts to block him out. He assumed the Captain's background never fully equipped him with the cultural and emotional discipline needed to hide emotions. It was common knowledge that Beydo had worked his way up from very humble roots, both socially and professionally, attaining Executive Status and the responsibility for an entire world's law enforcement. He was clearly unhappy that Central Government had sent an agent from the Specialist Assignments Unit and he was likely to view the interference as a slight due to his Worker Class background.

Glancing back at the shuttle, Higani watched the forward access ramp lower and noted two motionless figures at the top, amid the crew's flurry of movement as they prepared for disembarkation. They stood in the standard dark formal suits expected of plain-clothed agents, the larger of the two shielding his eyes from the bright sunlight after close to three weeks under artificial light. The other appeared shorter, though it was difficult to tell from a distance as he stood slightly hunched, shielding his face with a wide brimmed hat as he tried to light a nictostick in the brisk morning wind.

"The bastard's 'ave sent two of 'em," Beydo complained angrily.

"No," Higani said thoughtfully, "The big man, he's muscle, bodyguard probably. The other man, he's the one you'll need to watch. Beydo grunted while Higani pointed out the rifle case the big man carried as the pair started to walk down the ramp.

"Come," Beydo ordered, turning to face the lounge door, "We'll meet 'em back at headquarters."

The Interrogator

The assassins thankfully botched their initial attack and missed me totally. Jorich was not so lucky, the slugs from all three machine guns spun him across the walkway like a scrunched up Happy Snax wrapper. I managed to dive behind this wall leaving Jorich sprawled out on his back, out in the open and just out of reach. There was nothing I could do but hunch down and escape this barrage of metal, brick and wood-chip. Strange isn't it, how time slows in situations like this. Was it really only seconds ago that I watched my partner's laboured breathing? Watched helplessly as it brought blood gurgling and foaming up over his quivering lips as he slowly bled out across the street.

Eight hours earlier

Sam watched Jorich chew the side of his index finger as they walked down the ramp. In his free hand, he carried the rifle case containing his favourite blaster. Sam had to grin and shaking his head, he told the big man that he should have left his rifle with the rest of their luggage.

"You know me better than that," his partner replied, "Anyway, I don't trust this place, I mean look at that." Sam enjoyed Jorich's disgust at the police transport that awaited them at the foot of the ramp, "I mean, it's got wheel's, it's a bloody a ground car."

"This is a backwater planet Jorich." Sam's placating nasal voice did little to improve his partner's mood, "Low population, and only one city to speak of. There's probably not much in way of tech, not outside of food production at any rate."

"Humph!" Jorich grunted, "Then why are we here?" Sam suggested the usual... politics.

"I bet they got a VTOL someplace. It's a bloody liberty, that's what it is."

8

The Interrogator

"How long?" I subvocalize into my imbedded jaw mic.

"ETA three minutes," a controller's measured voice replies, causing my skull to slightly vibrate behind my right ear.

"I might not have that long."

The terrorists are out of time, they have to act now, press the attack or withdraw before the SNAP squad arrives. What they do next will tell me something about who these assassins are. Fanatics, driven by ideology and purpose, will press the attack. Professionals, on the other hand, will withdraw now, while they still can and regroup to live and try another day. I hope for the latter as I will surely not survive a direct attack on my own. I might take out one or two but the third will no doubt survive to kill me.

Six hours earlier

Beydo sat at his desk in shirt sleeves and made no attempt at courtesy. He ignored the smaller man's hand when he offered it and stared up at his newly arrived guests in smug defiance. The big man barely noticed, he just casually looked around, the rifle bag still tightly gripped in his gorilla like fist. Higani knew what he was, his surface thoughts confirmed what the man's build and demeanour had already suggested. He would mention it to Beydo later. The other man, to his credit, was able to hold The Captains gaze. He was almost as tall as his partner but hid it well behind a stooped posture. Higani suspected he wasn't as physically weak as his countenance suggested. There was something of the weasel about him, Higani thought, as he watched him hold The Captain's gaze with dark intelligent eyes. He was middle aged, with dark thinning hair, a long rat like face and small piercing eyes. The man spoke mainly through his nose, his voice high pitched, almost a whine as he introduced himself as Specialist Agent Samet Dapes. His partner was just Jorich. Higani noted that Dapes was extremely calm, despite Beydo's provocation. There was also a lack of emotional bleed that only came with formal training and absolute discipline.

"So Captain," The weasel continued pleasantly, "how can we help?"

The Interrogator

A lull in gun fire. They've messed up. All reloading at once, I hope. I stand, aim and fire. One is running, one is reloading and one is standing still, a neat hole between her eyes, the scarf that had hidden her nose and mouth slowly unwraps and falls to the ground. No blood, the wound cauterized by the laser. Her companion looks at me and raises his weapon, a split second distraction as he sees his compatriot sink to her knees. That split second is enough. He drops the machine gun as his right arm falls limp and useless at his side, the shoulder destroyed by three grouped laser holes. I break cover and walk toward my attackers. The fleeing assassin is almost at the corner. A kneecap explodes out from a laser shot to the back of his leg. He falls, weapon clattering to the ground out of reach. The second assassin is clumsily scrambling for his weapon with his offhand now, I don't need both of them alive so he is neatly taken out with a head shot. The third assassin loses his other good knee and collapses around the corner almost out of sight. I watch his useless legs slowly disappear as the poor bastard tries to drag himself away. No rush, he's not going anywhere fast.

Five hours earlier

Sam sat in the back of the police transport as it sped along the freeway towards the city's affluent suburbs. Jorich sat next to him, gazing absent minded out of the window, rifle case held firmly on his lap. They were travelling fast along the express lane reserved for diplomats, politicians and emergency vehicles. Not quite in the farming districts, the scenery was mainly billboards and the occasional glimpse of a tenement block.

"Nice town," Jorich observed as his head slowly turned with each billboard as they passed, "quiet, not too grimy, this should be a cake run." Sam wasn't so sure.

Slowly the billboards and buildings thinned out and the two agents found themselves glimpsing patches of green as they passed woodland, field and Municipal Park. Side roads branched off left and right, each one leading off to semi-automated farm complexes or large and gaudy mansions.

The mansions belonging to the rich and famous of Cass III were all ornate and unique expressions of wealth and status. Sam hated them. To his 'core world' sensitivities, they all looked provincial and vulgar.

"That one looks like a castle," Jorich said, almost excitedly, "It's got turrets and everything."

"Yes Jorich how wonderful for you," Sam was instantly annoyed at himself for his patronising tone.

The big man didn't seem to notice. It wasn't the great lummox's fault, it was just the way he was made. Sam usually welcomed the brute's naive simplicity, finding it refreshing, especially in their line of work. "And look there Jorich," Sam softly added, sincere now, no longer ridiculing, "That one is made of glass, it is completely transparent."

"I wouldn't like that," The big man snorted, "I like a bit of privacy when I'm having a shit."

Regardless of design and individualism, each mansion had one thing in common, large landscaped gardens behind high ironstone walls with tall foreboding plexisteel gates. The transport veered left and took a side road up towards one of those gates.

The Interrogator

I guess it's the adrenaline, I didn't hear the sirens, the screech of tires on tarmac, not until now, not until I hear somebody calling my name.

"Agent Dapes! Hold up please."

I turn. It is that supercilious Esper Lieutenant. He asks me what happened. I shrug and tell him we were ambushed. I continue towards the corner knowing he will follow. He asks how this could have happened. I shrug again. That is of course the same question playing on my mind. Why here? Why now? Who knew we were going to be here, without back-up at this precise time. I ask the Esper those very questions. He says he doesn't know and pretends not to understand what it is I am really inferring. The hidden question. Who's the traitor in his department?

We reach the corner. I am impressed, the assassin has crawled further than I had expected. He looks back at me over his shoulder, mask discarded. I can almost taste his fear. No real need for accuracy now, not at this range. I look at the Esper, hold eye contact as I alter my laser pistol's lens setting to a wide beam. I breathe slowly, making myself calm, I clear my mind. I don't want him to read me, I want to appear cold, as emotionless as stone. I want this man to understand what it is I am. Scare him, make him drop his guard.

I turn and fire. The assassin's right foot disintegrates. I suspect he has fainted, he had looked close to it. I did not wait to see, I have already turned back to look at the Esper's shocked face, colour draining from his thin face. I allow a thin smile. I've got him. He knows something about that man.

"We need to get him back for questioning," I tell him.

To be continued.

13

The Merging of Thear's Two Moons
Regina Puckett

May the union of Zosarah and Oxseth bring the warring moons of Picexan and Zo together in peace forever and always.

Zosarah

"I thought I would find you here."

Zosarah tightened the strap on her dardlizz's saddle before looking up at her mother. She needed that extra time to rein in her anger. After all, it wasn't her mother's fault she had been sacrificed to stop a war between Picexan and Zo, but while she understood the need for the treaty and the forced marriage to a man she had never met before, it still irked that her father had done so without first consulting her. Of course, the outcome would still have been the same, but she might not have felt so utterly betrayed by his decision to barter his only child like mere livestock.

"I thought I would make use of what little freedom I have left." A note of bitterness crept into her last few words. Zosarah bowed her head so her mother wouldn't see the unwelcome tears.

"Your father's worried you now hate him. I reassured him you understand your duty to the people of Picexan." Queen Bethelisa placed her hand over the one Zosarah had rested on her dardlizz's neck.

Her mother's ice cold touch did nothing to relieve Zosarah's anxiety, but she met Queen Bethelisa's eyes with a confidence she far from felt. "Of course I will. It's what we royals always do after all, isn't it? We serve our subjects and do what is best for them. I know my duty, Mother. I just don't like it."

"Maybe when you say those same words to your father later, you'll sound more sincere than you do now." Even though Queen's Bethelisa's voice was firm, her eyes held only kindness and understanding for her daughter's predicament. "My only consolation is that you will only be a day's journey away. Though I knew this day would come, I still find myself unprepared to have you even that small distance from me."

Zosarah resisted the temptation to roll her eyes. Even though the queen was her mother, she was still the queen. Besides, maybe there was still a slight chance of changing her father's mind. It might work to her favor to play the ever-obedient daughter.

"What do you know of this Zoan you have pledged me to?" How could her parents have bartered her away to such a barbaric realm? "I always thought, even if I never loved who I was bound to, that at least I might one day come to love him. How will that be possible when I'll be caged for the rest of my life, as if I'm some lowly beast?" She patted her dardlizz's purple leathery neck. Its rough feel matched her cantankerous mood.

16

She had no intention of being caged for the people of Picexan or for her father.

Much to Zosarah's surprise, her mother laughed.

"You still believe in that myth? Those tales of the Zoan are only told as a way of keeping Picexan children in check." The queen crossed her arms. Now nearing dusk, ice shards had begun to fill the air and a few had settled on the ends of her long green hair. They sparkled in the fading light. "The Zoans are just as civilized as the Picexans."

"Then why are we heading toward a war with them?" As long as Zosarah could remember, they had always been on the verge of it with the Zoan's.

"Because both the Zoans and the Picexans can be stubborn and hardheaded." The queen let out a long and weary sigh. "Your father hopes your marriage to King Oxseth will settle the matter once and for all. No king wants unrest. Your father knows, even though you can be temperamental and hardheaded, that you can also be kind and endearing. He hopes the Zoan's will love you just as much as our own people do."

The huge dardlizz stomped its rear feet – a warning it was tiring of standing in one place for too long.

Zosarah patted its neck and placed her foot in the stirrup. "I promise I'll be back in time for tonight's marriage announcement." The last thing she wanted was to miss meeting her soon to be mate. There were a few things she needed to get straightened out before the vow ceremony.

"Don't be late, and do something with your hair before you make an appearance at court." Queen Bethelisa stepped back from the dardlizz, wary of its ten razor sharp wings. Zosarah's dardlizz was well-trained to keep them at rest until otherwise instructed, but it was, after all, a wild beast at heart.

Zosarah mounted, anxious to get out of the stuffy stall and to feel the Picexan's cold, ice-filled air against her pale green skin. The pain would remind her she wasn't dead yet, that there was still time to figure a way out of her predicament.

"I promise to be so beautiful that the King of Zo will weep from want."

"Well spoken, Daughter. I always knew you would make a great queen one day." Bethelisa moved to leave but paused long enough to add, "One day, the Zoan's will love you so much they'll forget they ever hated the people of Picexan."

Zosarah laughed. "I'm afraid that you and my father's love has put the very survival of Picexan and Zo on my shoulders. I'm not certain I'm worthy of such trust, or if I'm up to such an enormous task."

"It will give you something to think about while you're out riding."

"And all I wanted to do was to forget everything for a little while." For a moment Zosarah couldn't breathe. Her parents were expecting too much of her. Was she really unselfish enough to throw her life away for her people?

She pressed her heels into the flanks of the dardlizz and tried to blank out her fears for a while. Only time would tell what her future would hold.

"Stand still. You're making me dizzy."

"I bloody well won't stand still until I see the wench my father has betrothed me to." Oxseth pulled at his freshly pressed collar and fought the urge to jump on his gleae and fly as far away as soon as he could from this ice filled moon. How could anyone stand these shards of ice floating through the air they breathed? The Zosarahs must be the toughest race he had even met. How was he supposed to mate with such a creature?

Oxseth shuddered. Every time he shook hands with King Lilipph it took ages for his own to warm up again. How was he supposed to bed a wife who had ice running through her veins?

All out of patience, Oxseth's valet threw down his clothing brush. "Fine. Go out looking like a peasant. You've only yourself to blame."

"Maybe I'll be so hideous the king's daughter will refuse me a union." He snapped his fingers. "That's it. I'll be so obnoxious and boorish she will refuse me."

Oxseth slapped his leg. "There's got to be a better way to settle our disagreement than joining my life to one of these cold-blooded, barbaric people."

"If you didn't want to marry the king's daughter, then why did you agree to go along with his idea in the first place? I'm certain the two of you could have found a way of lessening tension between our peoples besides a bonding with his daughter. It's never been done before, you know. What if you can't produce an heir with her?"

Oxseth duly noted that his longtime valet and friend had enough common sense to take a step back – just enough to be safely out of harm's way. It was tempting to backhand Retwal for reminding him of his most recent error in judgement. Oxseth hated to admit that his friend had a good point. What if this coupling didn't produce an heir, and how could it? The Picexan's were cold-blooded and the Zoan's warm. And how did this whole coupling thing work with a Picexan anyway? He was going to look a bloody fool if he did the wrong thing.

"Bloody hell," and Oxseth sat on the nearest surface.

"What's wrong now?" Retwal came over and placed a hand on his shoulder. "Please tell me you're not going to lose your meal, not so soon before meeting your new mate to be?"

Oxseth pushed Retwal's hand away and stood. "Let's just get this over with. If she turns out to be some hideous creature, we'll make a run for our gleaes and prepare for war."

"You would draw your subjects into a war for such a selfish reason?"

"Of course not, but for a moment the thought of running away like a coward lifted my spirits." He placed a hand on his friend's shoulder. "Some days I wish I had been born a commoner."

"You know as well as I do that wishes are only for fools, and not for kings."

Oxseth nodded. "Knowing it and accepting it are two entirely different things, my friend."

Zosarah

Even after an icy cold, refreshing shower, piling her long green hair on top of her head so her slender neck would be shown at its best and dressed in her prettiest gown, Zosarah still felt unprepared to face her future mate. The long flight through Picexan's darkening skies had done nothing to settle her nerves, but somewhere during that much needed get away she had decided to do as her father wished. How would she ever live with herself if her subjects had to go to war just because she didn't want to do her duty? It was why she had been born, to carry on her father's work. She had always thought that meant she would rule over Picexan, but instead, she would be living out her remaining days on its twin moon. How many times through her childhood had her father told her life wasn't fair. Such simple words that had held no real meaning until today.

Straightening her shoulders, Zosarah looked at her reflection one last time before running for the door. Her mother was going to kill her. She was already late to her own party. Her mother was at this very moment probably thinking she had run away. It was a wonder the queen hadn't already sent someone out looking for her. No matter. She was a fast runner. With any luck she would make it to the grand hall before scouts were sent out to drag her there like some wayward child.

Zosarah bound down the hallway and out into the courtyard, as if the fiery creatures from the underworld were nipping at her heels. She was running so fast when a tall figure stepped out directly into her path, that she had no other choice but to plow right into it. She would have fallen if two steel-like hands hadn't grabbed her shoulders and steadied her.

Too embarrassed to do anything, Zosarah stepped back and stared at her feet. "I'm so sorry," she whispered. My mother keeps telling me I have the grace of an elkle. I guess she's right."

A blue hand lifted Zosarah's chin, large blue eyes staring down at her. She again took a step back. "Thank you for your help, but my mother's going to have me flayed if I don't arrive soon."

Zosarah offered her hand to the huge Zoan. Could this be the man she was betrothed to? She swallowed past a lump in her throat. He was enormous. One swipe from his hand would surely kill her. While that thought should have frightened her, it did the opposite. A thrill of excitement ran through her as an unbidden picture flashed into her mind: his hands roving all over her.

She must have made some sort of sound because he stepped nearer and asked, "Are you hurt?"

Fortunately, before she could further embarrass herself, her mother's voice cut through the tense air. "So there you are, Daughter. I see you and King Oxseth have finally met."

There was something very satisfying about the stranger's surprised but pleased expression. Maybe, just maybe, this wasn't going to be as awful as Zosarah had at first feared.

"Are you running away from your marriage vows so soon?"

Zosarah paused, mid-step. Her internal argument lasted only a second before she gathered the gilded sheer layers of her gown and turned. After so many years of practicing diplomacy, it was easy to smile even when she didn't feel like it.

"I'm going to ride my dardlizz before the air becomes too thick with ice. Being a wife is new to me. I'm not used to asking permission before doing something so simple."

"Is it the custom of your world to ask your husband's permission before each and every decision?"

Icy fog hazily surrounded the newly married couple and settled on the outer layers of their clothes, and at the ends of Zosarah's long green hair. The ice shards on her hands reflected the flames of nearby lanterns. Even that brilliant sight, though, was nothing to compare to the spark of rebellion in her eyes.

Zosarah crossed her arms and lifted her chin. "Of course not, but it's my understanding that it is customary on Zo, and that all wives are kept locked in cages. I wanted one night of freedom before that became my fate."

Oxseth leaned forward, his face now just inches from hers. "The people of Zo cherish their women and children."

Something about his gentle tone caused her to relax her stance. "Would you like to ride along with me? I have heard many tales of how fast your gleaes can fly."

"That is what you wish to do on your wedding night? I can think of better things."

Zosarah's shrug was casual but her smile was filled with mischief. "There will be time enough to consummate our vows. We know so little of one another. If we don't trust each other then how will our people learn to trust the two of us to rule over them? I was thinking, perhaps, of a small challenge we could have between us, one that would help build some much needed faith in each other."

Oxseth shifted closer and placed a callused blue hand on her arm. "A challenge?"

She didn't shrug his hand off, but moved away enough that it fell of its own accord. "A race. If I win, I may pull a feather from the plumage of your gleae. If you win, you may ask for anything you desire."

His expression darkened. "You know so little about the nature of gleaes. They are vain beasts. If you were to win, my gleae would slice through me with its stinger. As my wife, how could you wish such a horrible death on me? Hours of unrelenting agony before I would die from its venom."

This time Zosarah was the one to move closer. She placed a hand on that of her new mate. "Trust me."

Oxseth bowed his head as he considered her challenge. He finally met her eyes and nodded. "Lead the way. You set the rules, and we'll see which one of us will win this race of yours. I always do what is best for my people, and now I'll also do what is best for you and the people of Picexan."

As soon as they were on their beasts and into the air, Zosarah pointed toward the edge of her kingdom. "The winner will be the first one to reach the darkness beyond the city's walls."

Oxseth eyed the great distance before sitting up straighter in his saddle, his face filled with confidence. "I hope you are well-rested, my love, because I will soon claim my prize."

His words sent a thrill through her, and so Zosarah bowed her head to keep him from reading her thoughts. She hoped he would think it meant she had already accepted defeat, not that she was looking forward to their first coupling. Shaking off her weakness at the thought, she lightly tapped her dardlizz's flanks. It immediately raised all ten of its wings and leapt higher into the air, cutting through the shards of ice around them as it raced toward the city's dark edge. She was there first and tugged on its reins, soon speeding back toward Oxseth. Before he could do a thing, she plucked the longest feather from his gleae's plumage. As expected, it lashed out and struck Oxseth with its powerful stinger.

She caught him before he could fall from his saddle and tucked him in front of her, whispering in his ear, "You have much to learn about me, my dear mate. I'm amazed at how much I'm looking forward to teaching you how to please a Picexan."

Hours later, she sat poised on the railing of their marriage bed.

Oxseth moaned and opened one eye. "I am not dead!"

"You're not."

He struggled to sit up but finally gave in and settled his head onto his pillow. "I don't understand."

"A dardlizz possesses an anti-venom for a gleae's sting. It will reverse the effects of its poison within a matter of a few hours. I set up this challenge so you would know you can always trust me with your life. The people of Zo and Picexan have no reason not to trust us to lead them. We can work together in all things, and we will always do what is right for us and for them."

Ozseth lifted himself onto his elbow and quirked an eyebrow. "Shall we race again?"

She stood and slipped the long layers of her silk gown over her head. The garment dropped, pooling around her bare feet. "Is that what you wish to do on your wedding night? I can think of better things."

The End

Red Moon Rising
By Ray Foster

Under a clear blue sky the landscape hummed with the soft sounds of insects. Somewhere, in the lush green grass crickets clicked, bees buzzed amongst the cornflowers while dragonflies hovered over the reeds that grew from the small stream that ran parallel to the empty road.

For a brief moment of time the natural sounds seemed to stop and hold its breath in anticipated expectation. Then the silence was broken by a distant hum that grew in volume to a raw powered roar as the customised Harley Davidson trike crested the rise.

The sun struck the brilliant chrome sparking out slivers of silver that speckled the road and grass verge. Nature returned to its natural chorus now joined by the soft clicking of the cooling engine.

The black clad rider absorbed all this in as he slipped a battered cheroot from the top pocket of his leather jacket and slid it, thoughtfully, between his lips before applying the flame from a red, disposable lighter to the tip.

Through narrowed eyes he peered beyond the haze of swirling blue smoke at the scene before him. He traced the gentle curve of black tarmac until it disappeared behind the bulk of a small church that dominated the bend. Opposite the tall stack of a former tin or copper mine stood guard at the cliff's edge below which, just visible, was a hint of green blue sea.

From this vantage point he could see the remains of a community that had once thrived here – all that remained were moss covered foundations of the cottages that had lined the road. Another short terrace of stone built houses peered out from behind the church.

This reverie was brought to an abrupt end as he caught sight of the corner of a car boot that was almost hidden by the chapel wall. He narrowed his eyes as he focused on the inverted 'Y' of the rear lights. It had been a long time since he had last seen an old Ford Cortina and curiosity made him wonder what it was doing here.

It was the little things like this that made him wary – there was the possibility of, at least, five people down there that would be interested in the contents of the box fitted at the rear of the trike. Therein lay a problem for on the one hand he needed to take a break while on the other there was always the prospect of a chase – and he did not fancy the latter.

Carefully, he slipped a sawn down shotgun from the holster tied down against his left thigh and checked the load before reaching into a saddlebag for a Colt M1911. He tucked the handgun into the belt at the small of his back then releasing the brakes he let the Harley roll, silently, down the road.

Halting close to the church door he slid from the saddle. Approaching with caution the door that stood ajar, he could hear a voice. A rough aggressive voice

28

demanded that someone stopped struggling and whatever was happening would be over quickly. Though the demands were not polite, just a bunch of expletives and derogatory terms that were underlined by what was seen as the biker stepped inside.

On the floor was a woman with an outstretched arm scrambling weakly to reach a knife that was beyond her reach. Astride her was an assailant, trousers down to his ankles and one hand wrapped around the woman's throat while the other ripped at her clothing.

The heavy built man had no inkling that he was being watched or that the woman had stopped struggling. He was in a world of his own as two shotgun barrels emptied their load into the side of his head. A kick of a boot sent the rest of the body to fall clear of his intended victim.

The killer emptied the shotgun, reloaded it and snapped the weapon shut. All this as his eyes looked around the church seeking signs of danger. Only when he was satisfied that there was only him did he drop to one knee beside the girl – for girl was all she seemed and one who appeared to be in her teens. Erring on the side of caution he kicked the knife further from her reach. Placing two fingers against the side of her neck he detected a pulse and a sharp slap to her face forced air into her lungs as she gulped it in. Her eyes were wide with shock as she looked, with frightened eyes, around her.

"You're alive, kid," he murmured as he stood up and stepped away from her.

"Wha-what happened?" she gasped, rolling over and climbing to her knees. As she moved, so the remnants of her sweat shirt fell from one arm but made no attempt to cover herself.

The biker just shrugged. "The other feller just lost his head." Then pointed at her. "Think you might want to clean up – you're covered in shit."

Blank, uncomprehending eyes stared back at him.

"Shit happens when people die," he offered by way of explanation. "There's no dignity there." He pointed the shotgun at the corpse. "He alone or are there more?"

She shook her head as it dawned on the girl that the man before her presented no danger to her. Glancing down she saw the blood that was splattered across her chest and the stains that had soaked into her torn, ragged jeans.

"Are you an American?" she asked, while using the remains of her sweat shirt to wipe the blood from her face and body.

"Expecting them to come to save the day?" he laughed, derisively. "Only in books and movies, kid. Besides, I reckon they've got their own problems or were you too busy clubbing to watch the news?"

"No, mate," she snapped back. "Done with that after a friend of mine with a drink problem took too many legal highs. Anyway, who watches the news anymore – all you see is the many ways that people can kill each other. No, I escaped into the pretend world of 'Titanfall' not that you'd know what that is."

"What was your favourite lead-out?" he grinned. "Mine was the R-101C assault rifle."

She stared at him, mouth agape as she stopped rubbing herself down.

"Problem?" he asked.

"But you're...." she was about to point out.

"Fifty five," he supplied. "Accounts for my greying hair but doesn't bar me from gaming."

She shook her head. "I didn't mean....I just never thought...."

"Shut up, kid," he said, kindly. "Just go get yourself cleaned up while I get rid of the corpse."

For a moment he watched her pick up a back pack before she left the church to cross the road to walk down by the old mine workings. There was nothing self-conscious about her – it was as if she was used to walking around stripped to the waist. Short, slightly stocky with stark muscle definition and long black hair that tumbled with turquoise streaks over her shoulders – put him in mind of some of his favourite female wrestlers.

"By the way," he called out. "The name's John – John Keel."

"Whatever," she shrugged with a dismissive wave of her hand.

Dismissing her from his mind he got on with the task in hand. Grabbing the corpse by the legs he dragged it out of and around the church towards the small graveyard at the back. Finding a depression he left the body in it. Then set off to do a little exploration.

* * * * *

As she made her way down to the beach her thoughts turned to her saviour. There was something cold about him as though he did not care for human life – there was neither empathy nor sympathy. Yet for reasons that she could not fathom she felt that she could trust him.

She had never trusted Warren – the man who had tried to rape her. They had run as a gang and with the crisis going on they had looted and committed arson. Croydon had burned but unlike that August when Reeves store went up in flames during the riots there had been no one to fight the fires. It was only when things were falling apart that she was drawn back into the gang. The death of her boyfriend had turned her into a recluse but the prospect of death by plague had sent her back out on to the streets.

No one knew much about the plague – it just happened. A sniffle, a cough and within hours you were dead. Both she and Warren had watched their friends choke to death – no point getting them to the overfull hospitals where the staff were amongst the dead and the dying. Laughingly now, many waited for the dead to rise like it was a zombie apocalypse.

Yeah, she smiled, some zombie apocalypse – waste of a good chainsaw that.

Stripped down naked she waded into the sea to jump waves with a childish glee before diving in headfirst. She swam for a while, gliding across the water that scoured her body clean before turning to float on her back.

Her thoughts drifted back to Warren – he had never been her type but, then, nor had his father. The teachers had known, the police had known and the authorities had too. Warren's father had a history of abusing young girls – but no one could touch him because he was a grass. Nor had her parents been much help – her abuser was family so you don't grass them up.

Until today, Warren, had never made any move towards her. He knew what his father had done but he had never been able to stand up to him. Warren, alone, was a scared little boy and that was why they ran from Croydon. They had no idea where they were going or why – and they had finished up here.

That was when Warren had lost it. He was scared of dying and never having had sex – she could not believe it. He was twenty six and still a virgin but he was her cousin and she couldn't – no wouldn't – give in to him.

Now they were all gone.

She laughed.

They were all punished in the end.

Now there was a new man around and he aroused her curiosity. If he turned out to be one of the good guys then he would have to earn her trust. That he had saved her was one thing but people don't do that without some ulterior motive. Two things that she was sure of, though, was that he was not looking for a daughter figure any more than she was looking for the father equivalent.

She waded from the sea and squatted on a rock where she had parked her back. After fiddling around inside, she produced a pair of scissors with which she attacked her jeans by cutting off the legs.

* * * * *

It was the last thing that John Keel needed – he didn't want to be lumbered with some teenage kid. So what if they had a connection via a computer game? That didn't make them best buddies or anything. It wasn't as if...

Face it, a voice inside his head prompted, you still think you are responsible for the deaths of your wife, your kids and grandkids. There was nothing you could do... nothing at all. 'So why did I live while they died?'

He thought that he had screamed those last words

out loud.

There had been nothing that he could do even if he had known how to.

The world was dying. Those that survived flocked towards city centres where they died at the hands of gangs or diseases spread by decaying corpses that littered the streets. Chaos ensued and he had known that sooner rather than later he would have to get away. He had a destination in mind but had no idea how to get there. Just a childhood memory to hang on to – all those holidays in Cornwall. It made him glad, in a way that his parents had been spared all this.

The trike had been his first find. It had been sitting on a garage forecourt with the owner slumped close to the pumps. Probably had died just after filling up and heading for the pay point. Although he had to make several detours, he made it to Heathrow Airport where he searched for members of the Transport Police. He stripped them of their Heckler & Koch semi-automatic carbines, ammunition and a couple of vests that he carried back to the trike and stored away in the box at the back. After strapping on a holster around his waist he checked that the Glock 17 pistol had a full load. Although he had not handled a gun since his days with the Air Training Corps everything that he knew about guns came flooding back.

But he had not been alone at the airport – there were others around and he knew that there was no time to negotiate. Two men died and he had an extra handgun and a sawn down shotgun. The man with the sawn down double-barrelled shotgun had looked like a movie-style Mexican bandit with crossed bandoliers of shotgun cartridges.

Keel had not hung around after that but took off westward. The only time he stopped after that was to raid a camping shop for a few odds and ends. The journey was not so straight forward for there were roaming gangs around to be avoided. A couple of villages were fortified but whether the defenders were friend or foe he wasn't prepared to discover. Habitation was to be avoided.

Instead of dwelling on the past he began to think of the present.

One by one he investigated the three cottages by the side of the church. The first was run down and musty smelling but the second had been lived in. There was furniture: table and chairs in front of a small range and a lantern hung from a hook and chain that was nailed to a beam along the ceiling. The sole kitchen cupboard revealed a stash of tinned food most of which was still in date and hinted that someone had lived there. Only the cold embers in the stove bore testament that it had not been used in quite a while.

The end cottage proved to contain a surprise for it revealed itself to be a fully functioning blacksmiths, though the forge was as cold as the stove next door. As he was about to leave he saw a fishing net that brought back childhood memories.

Armed with net, a bucket and a billy can he set off for the beach.

***

He saw her lying on a rock and smiled as he shook his head. It seemed an impossible scene with her stretched out naked, her weight balanced on her elbows, letting the sun dry her. He started to turn away just as she twisted around to look at him but he ignored

35

her to get on with the task in hand. He walked around the rocks at the other end of the beach, set the billy down before filling the bucket with sea water. Once done he set about scouring the sand with the net. It took ten minutes for him to find the first prawns, their grey shells covered in seaweed. After scooping them into the bucket he trawled a different area and gleaned a larger harvest. Only when he had enough to feed them both did he stop to fill the billy with sea water from a clear pool.

Another time and he would have searched for crab and lobster – it would be just a matter of tracking down those secret places where they hid.

"What on earth are you doing?" the girl demanded, as she approached him.

"Getting us something to eat," he mentioned, setting everything down and looking around for some driftwood.

"Really?" her eye brows rose. "You expect me to eat that?" she peered into the bucket. "God, they're still alive."

"Which means they're fresh," he responded, scooping up some dried grass and twigs. "Make yourself useful and see if you can find some wood."

For a moment she looked ready to protest then turned away to do as he had asked. He watched her go and couldn't help but think that there was a change in her.

She was now dressed in grey denim cut-offs, pink and white knee length socks tucked into a pair of old army boots and an urban camouflaged sports bra that should have laced up over her chest – but didn't. Her hair had been tied back so tightly that it made her face look hard.

As soon as she returned, Keel built a fire and put the billy on. They sat side by side and watched the water bubble away as the prawns turned pink.

"How do you know how to do all this?" she asked as she peeled and ate her first prawn.

"Learned from my dad," Keel reminisced. "We spent all our holidays down here. He taught me how to fish, look for prawns, crabs and lobsters – and how to cook them."

"You've got good memories," she said sadly as she half rose then sat back down again. "I suppose you're going to move on?"

Keel shook his head. "Comes a time when I need to stop running and I guess you can take care of yourself. Stay or go it makes no difference to me."

"I wondered when you were going to come down to basics," she sneered. "Go on hit me with your best shot – we are the future of mankind. Right?"

"Wrong," he snapped straight back. "We cocked up the world already; you think that I want to start the whole thing over again? Sorry, girl mankind can go to hell for all I care as long as they don't drag me down with them."

"Wow!" was her surprised response. "That's not what I expected. I never wanted kids anyway and definitely not in this world. What life would it have?"

"This is true," he nodded.

For a while they sat silently, both lost in their thoughts as they stared out towards the horizon. The afternoon drifted into early evening and with it came a chill in the breeze. As she shivered, so Keel removed his leather jacket and placed it around her shoulders.

"I got sacked from my last job," she said, breaking the silence. "I trained at college as a brickie – they said that I'd never cope so I used to work out at the gym. I was good at my job and took all the insults. Then the summer came and there they were all stripped to the waist showing off their abs and tats. I took it all in my stride until it all got too much – probably due to the monthly visit – and I just stripped off my top and worked topless. They just stood there and gaped when they got a good look at me. So I got sacked for showing them up. They called me Dirty Nicole and the name stuck – all that training and I couldn't get work."

"They felt threatened," Keel pointed out. "The difference is that I don't."

To emphasise the point he slipped the Colt from his waistband and placed it, butt towards her, on the rock between them.

"What's that for?" she asked, suspiciously.

"Better learn how to handle that – for starters." He was serious. "Doesn't pay to take a knife to a gunfight."

She picked it up and examined it.

"Britt did and he won," Nicole grinned, wickedly. "Or have you never seen 'The Magnificent Seven'?"

"Touché, kid," Keel nodded.

"Just don't call me that," she suggested. "I'm not a kid. This thing started on my 20th birthday."

"Fair enough," there was a promise in his voice.

* * *

In the early hours of the morning, after a restless sleep filled with nightmare scenes, Keel woke up and stepped out of the church. The moon hung huge, red and menacing over the sea. He became aware that he was not alone.

"What does it mean?" Nicole asked. "Is it really a sign of bad things?"

He simply nodded: "There's a war coming and we're going to have to get ready for it."

The End

The Story of the Goat who gets the Gold
By Kalyan Mattaparthi

The elderly gent in the saloon, had not yet taken notice of this little drama. The boar had since moved off, to paths unknown while the horse had been watching and cheering. Offering whinnies and calls for the victorious brown, leather snatcher.

Soon the gunslinger and goat were once again launching themselves past each other. One trying to capture, the other escaping. At one point, the little goat dashed under the porch planks, just out of the man's reach. Poking her head out now and again, she teased the human with his own leather.

While under the porch, she tripped on a small pouch and bent down to investigate. She picked it up, and while the man was catching his breath. She took the pouch onto the porch. She sat down, and while still holding the strip of leather, tried to rip open the pouch.

She became intent upon it and very curious about its contents.

So hypnotised was she by it, that she didn't see the man coming closer to her with a most unfriendly look on his dust covered face. He slowly snuck up, and when close enough, he grabbed for the pilfered strap seizing it in luscious triumph.

At that same moment, the goat had worked a hole into the pouch. When the man yanked the leather from the jaws of the bothersome animal, three small shiny yellow nuggets fell from the bag plunking neatly onto the wood deck.

Both characters stopped their pursuits to take a moment's notice of this. The eyes of the man widened, as he recognized the golden stone. The nostrils of the goat flared, at this new questioning thing. The two then looked at each other, and the goat leaped back with the bag of nuggets tightly held in her mouth, when she realized how close the human had come.

In the distance, the horse had found much enjoyment in watching these two combatants but was now tired and had pandered off to his stall. In the saloon, the aged barkeep was entertaining a local doctor. They were discussing marital relations, and bovine acquisitions, giving little, if any, notice to the drama just outside. A bleat from the goat did prompt a moment's pause in the conversation, querying as to whether there was a sheep herder in town but the two soon continued on their previous topics.

Returning to the event on the porch, our gunslinger was now down on one knee. Tentatively holding out the now drool and dust covered bit of leather trying to entice the goat, hoping to gain the bag of found stones. The goat, still very attached to its new treasure, turned, and let out an ill wind, pointedly refusing the offer.

"Come on. You wanted this, right?" tempted the gunslinger.

"Baa," and a bit of gas, was the refused response.

"Well, I never..." exclaimed insulted human.

He made a grab for the legs of the critter. Successful, he pulled the hide legs till his arms were wrapped around the animal's middle. The wriggling creature managed to twist, and with one good kick, she got herself free, and left a neat hoof print smack in the middle of the gunslinger's forehead.

The goat, still in possession of the gold, made her way further down the saloon porch. She was now within range of the swinging doors. As the dishevelled and insulted gunslinger rushed for the goat. She darted under the doors of the saloon, and hid under a table.

Panting, she was very nervous, shaking under her table. For now she wasn't just hiding from the gunslinger, she was hiding from the barkeep. She knew if she stayed here too long, she might end up in a stew.

The gunslinger, with guns drawn once more, seemingly very determined to get the goat, or the gold, entered into the saloon. He peered into the establishment eagerly for his target.

The two men at the bar, had finally taken notice of the little event. They turned their attention to the gunslinger, and questioned his poised pistols.

The gunslinger realized where it was he found himself. Feeling suddenly tired from the taunting of the furry thief, he remembered that it was a saloon that he wanted, before this predicament began. So taking stock of the two others, he put away his guns, and bellied up to the bar.

The goat steadied herself, seizing her opportunity for freedom, dashed back under the doors. She quietly listened through a window, to make sure she was safe. For indeed she was, she could hear the three men begin a conversation.

Thus confident in her defeat of the gunslinger, she trotted off, holding the pouch of high. For the Goat had got away with the Gold.

The End

Chaos on Cass
By Chris Raven

Part Two: Investigation
Cass III (The Third Planet of the Eta Cassiopeiae System, 20LY from Sol and held in fealty for the Terran Star Empire by the Imperial House of Lein Rocha)

The Telepath

The prisoner is about to be loaded onto the back of the ambulance. I look back at the man who shot him, that rat faced individual in a wide brimmed hat and a thin nasally voice. Three times he shot the prisoner, by all accounts. Popped both kneecaps and disintegrated a foot. I witnessed that last act of cruelty myself. He took the man's foot for no other reason than to assert his authority, the cold bastard. It even took me twenty minutes to convince him to allow us to take his prisoner to the City General Hospital and only then on the promise we can question him there. Why can't I read this man? This Samet Dapes, an SAU agent from the Lein Rochan House Guard. I have never seen anyone so disciplined. I am a grade three telepath for Kristo's sake, no mundane should be able to block me out so effortlessly.

I follow Dapes' gaze down to his dead partner, the muscleman, still sprawled out on the walkway.

"Your partner," I say, "a bio-replicate isn't he? Military model I expect. I'm afraid we can't match that on our remanso planet. We could probably find you a spare labourer, if you wanted one."

There! Right there! Just for a second. A flash of anger. Dapes slowly looks up, a warm smile returning as the emotional void descends around him once again.

"Jorich?" he casually replies, "he was a specialist unit I'm afraid, I had him conditioned just so."

"That is a shame," I commiserate, "If you allow us a few days we could run you up something more sophisticated, a personal aide perhaps or a pleasure model if you prefer."

There again, for a second, less intense this time. Anger all the same and not just at me. There was some regret just then, maybe even grief. Well, well, well.

"That won't be necessary," The Specialist Agent pleasantly reassures as he turns away with a nonchalant shrug and walks towards a waiting patrol car.

Four hours earlier

Rosario Guzman liked to greet his guests in his well equipped kitchen. The Resident Chief Secretary to the Colonial Governor liked to cook, despite having what was universally agreed to be the best personal chef on the planet. Over his fifteen year political career, Guzman had served three different Governors for two separate Noble Houses and he had always found cooking a good way to reconnect to his roots. He had also found the practical routine a good way to manage stress. The dozen or so dishes of hot and cold food that covered the kitchen's sizable breakfast table was a testament to the amount of pressure he was currently under.

Guzman's guests were ushered into the kitchen, their presence announced by his head of staff quietly clearing his throat.

"Thank you Jaikab that will be all." Guzman turned to face his guests, the servant had already retreated from the room.

"Secretary Guzman?" A thin weasel of a man asked as he started to approach, hand outstretched. He was followed by a second much larger man, who seemed to carry what Guzman uncomfortably assumed was a rifle case.

"Please come in," Guzman invited, suspiciously eyeing the big man's case, "would you like me have a servant put that away for you?" The big man shook his head and grunted a no.

Guzman quickly wiped his palm on his overall and took the weasel's hand. As they shook, his guest commentated on his cooking.

"Yes, please help yourself to something," Guzman offered. The big man needed no second invitation and with one hand, he clumsily tucked in, his other hand never letting go of the rifle case. The weasel asked what each dish was before politely trying a small piece of one.

"This is Tapas," Guzman explained, "Have you tried it?" The weasel shock his head so Guzman explained that it was traditional Cassian cuisine. Small hot and cold snack foods made from various light ingredients, mainly cured meats and cheeses, seafood, some tomato and garlic based dishes, olives, herbs.

"The original colonists brought it with them," Guzman went on to explain, "although the recipes have evolved over the past nine hundred years or so, blending local and Terran ingredients."

Guzman paused to allow his guest to comment but the Weasel just stood there, face impassive and unreadable. Guzman shifted uncomfortably and noticed the agent's big accomplice eyeing him with amusement, picking at his teeth with his free hand. He felt even less reassured when the Weasel finally asked him how he might be of assistance.

The Telepath

I can feel the secret policeman's presence in the back of the patrol car. Nothing extrasensory, just his weight on the seat next to me, the sound of his breathing, slight movement caught in my vision's periphery. We are being taken to the hospital to interrogate the surviving terrorist, his compatriots slaughtered by the man who is now beside me. This thin, stooped, wiry man with the annoying voice. Nobody would look twice at him, as long as they did not know who he was. I suspect our prisoner will wish he had died with his friends before too long. Once Specialist Agent Samet Dapes is finished with him.

Yes, I am aware that he is there beside me, but I am used to sensing people both physically and psionically. This man, with his ability to shield his thoughts and emotions, he just feels like a ghost to me and like all ghosts should, he's scaring the shit out of me.

Four hours earlier

The Watcher watched Guzman from the light fitting above the breakfast table. He saw him squirm under the interrogator's gaze, while the other man, the bodyguard, seemingly unaware of the interaction, remaining preoccupied with the food, his gun case still firmly gripped in his left hand.

Guzman was speaking. Annoyed at not doing so earlier, the watcher pressed a key on his comp-pad and instantly heard the colonial secretary's pleading voice through his aural implant.

"So as you can see, it's a personal family matter that has merely gotten out of hand. I'm just sorry the affair has caused you and your colleague a wasted journey."

"Tell me more about your daughter's disreputable friends," The interrogator asked, his nasal voice friendly and polite.

"As I explained before," Guzman whined, stress beginning to show in his voice, "Mellissa, my daughter, out of rebellion more than anything else, has gotten herself involved with the political set at university, you know, older kids, that's all. She's just acting out, punishing me because I froze her allowance."

"I see," the interrogator prompted. Guzman licked his lips and helplessly looked at his two guests. The Watcher could see sweat forming and running down the side of his face.

"They're just kids," he pleaded, "taken things too far I grant you, but they're still just kids. Idealistic, naive, impulsive, we were teenagers once."

"True," the interrogator replied thoughtfully, "but I am sure your youthful high jinks fell short of kidnapping."

"Oh for Kristo's sake!" Guzman was getting frustrated now, "I told you, she's set it all up. It's all too convenient, don't you see? She's faked the kidnap to get her allowance back."

"So it's only extortion, is that what you are saying?"

"No!" Guzman's anger was barley disguising his fear, "Of course not. It really is a private matter and no concern of the Agency."

"The kidnapping of the daughter of a high ranking colonial official?" The interrogator turned to his colleague, "Wouldn't you say that this is exactly the sort of thing The Agency should be concerning itself with, eh Jorich?" The muscle man grunted back an affirmative.

"It's too hot to talk in here," Guzman complained, "I've been cooking all morning. If you insist on pursuing this pointless line of enquiry, at least let's do it in comfort."

The Watcher followed Guzman and his guests, jumping from light fitting to light fitting as they made their way through the mansion towards the main reception room. Guzman continued to protest his daughter's innocence by accusing her of duplicity, while the interrogator remained content to quietly listen. They were shown into a formal yet comfortable room, a place designed for entertaining officials and VIPs, with a well-stocked drinks cabinet, leather chairs and warm ambient lighting. Without seeking permission, the interrogator took a carton of nictosticks from his pocket and started to light one with a pocket igniter. The Watcher saw Guzman begin to protest but quickly think better of it.

"Would you like a drink?" he asked. Both guests declined, slowly shaking their heads.

"Now Administrator Guzman," The Interrogator continued, "shall we get on with this?"

The Telepath

The comp-pad vibrates in my breast pocket, as Agent Dapes' hand moves swiftly to his ear. He is getting an alert the same as me. I take the pad from my pocket and tap the screen to activate it. The message comes through the pad's speakers as the mug shots of three young adults scroll across it. The terrorists have been identified. Dapes is listening intently, staring blankly ahead, eyes flickering. I assume he is studying the same pictures via an optical implant.

"Kristo!" He turns to me and for the first time since making planetfall, he appears uncomfortable, "The woman I killed," he says, "It was her, the daughter, it was Melissa Guzman."

To be continued.

Outpost 223
By Dani J Caile

Why oh why I was out here on this stinky little outpost on the rim of our civilised universe, I shall never know. They said I'd be paid well, they said I'd be a hero when I get back, blah, blah, blah. But after nine months ticking boxes and filing analyses, the incessant screen watching and display checks were screwing up my brain, what with me all alone, only the clicks and beeps to keep me company. I was starting to look forward to the weekly status reports. The next one was due in four days and my legs were getting edgy, making me walk up and down past display after display of readouts, numbers and fancy lights signifying chemical compounds and their ratios in the space outside.

Three o'clock, time for tea. Only my watch kept some normality in my mind, keeping me regular. Seven o'clock up, have breakfast, start checking. Twelve, lunch, three, tea, eight, dinner and ten o'clock back to bed. Every day. For nine months. And what was there to check? Nothing, a big nothing. They hadn't actually specified as to what I was checking for but they said I'd know when I'd found it. Well, I'd found something but it wasn't what I'd expected. It was an urge to go home.

I hadn't left home the best way. I'd accumulated a large gambling debt and ran away, leaving my wife and kids to fend for themselves while I dodged the local villain who'd allowed me to borrow 'just a little more' until it was time to smash my knees. I needed a way to make money and make it quick, so when I saw the advert in the paper asking for "Deep Space Analysers", with 'excellent pay and health plan', I grabbed at the chance. And so did they. Not many people wanted the job and now I can see why. At least my family was now living the good life back home. I wish I was there. Three more months to go.

"Richard, are you okay?"

Oh yes, I forgot to mention. Technically, I wasn't alone, there was the main computer, Ákos IV. I think I understand what happened to the first three.

"Yes, Ákos, I'm fine."

"Would you like some anti-depressants or uppers? I can create some using the..."

"No, no, Ákos, I'm fine, really." I'd made the mistake about two months in, to accept this type of offer. I was out for a week, well, still working, my body was moving, I was checking, ticking away quite happily. Then I suffered from the side effects, the headaches, nausea, like a hangover with double gravity, the air pushing down on your brain.

"Would you like a nice cup of tea, then, Richard?"

"Yes, Ákos, I was just about to go have tea."

"It will be waiting for you at your console." And so it was.

"Ákos?"

"Yes, Richard?"

"Why are you called Ákos IV?" I liked to wind him up.

"That information is not within my data banks. If you'd like to ask another question, I'd be happy to answer it."

"Why is the sky blue?"

"Richard, you have asked me this question a million times and technically it is not blue, but..."

"Why do the trees move and shake in the wind?"

"Richard, I think you are forgetting that I am a computer and that as a computer I can only answer questions within the range of my programming."

"How many stars are there in the sky?" Its silence made my day. Perhaps I had gone a little nuts since being here, and perhaps it wasn't such a great idea to pick on the computer which controlled everything inside the outpost, including my life support systems, with juvenile, ridiculous questions. But I had to do something.

"Plus one." I spat out my tea.

"What?"

"Richard, there is plus one."

"Plus one what?"

"Plus one star. And it is becoming larger by the second. After further analysis, I can assume it not to be a star but a moving object of sorts, moving at an incredible rate of speed."

"What? Something is moving out there?"

"Everything is 'moving out there', Richard. Nothing is stationary. We are moving."

"I mean, there's something else out there?"

"Yes, Richard, and it's coming in this direction."

I slammed my tea down on the console and ran across the length of the displays and screens, searching for any evidence of what Ákos was saying. After frantically typing out some calculations and scribbling a few numbers down, there was nothing.

"Ákos, the scanners can't find anything."

"That is strange, Richard. I will recheck my systems. All okay. I am fine, Richard, and yet I am still sensing 'plus one' from the answer to your last irrelevant question." As Ákos's full stop hit, a large clang echoed through the building.

"What was that?" I stood still, hoping to hear it again, or maybe hoping not to.

"I am sorry, Richard, I do not know what you are referring to."

Another clang made me run straight towards the weapons locker.

"That, Ákos! That! What the hell was that?" Fumbling for the key, I dropped the whole set and was now on all fours poking through the floor framing, which covered all internal structure not on the main walkway, trying to find them.

"I am sorry, Richard but I have no idea as to what you are referring to."

After ripping off some skin from my fingers, I grabbed the keys, found the correct one and opened the weapons locker. One laser pistol, half charged. One lousy laser pistol. By the looks of it, at least twenty years old.

"Ákos! Is this it? Is this all there is in terms of weapons?"

"Other than my surface-to-space missiles, yes, Richard. Is there something wrong? Would you like an anti-depressant or...?"

"No! I'd like a bigger gun!"

"I will make a note of your requirement, Richard, for the next weekly status report."

Another clang, larger than the first two, sounded right above my head. I grabbed the pistol, and pressed 'kill' mode.

"Are you sure that is wise, Richard?"

"Look, if there's someone... or something out there, I want to be ready for the worst." My hands trembled as I looked around, wondering what would happen next. A loud beep from a display caught me off guard and I fired. The beep faded out and smoke filled the outpost.

"Richard, you destroyed one of the analysers."

"Yes, Ákos, thanks for that. I'm aware of what I did."

"I will need to add that to the weekly status report, Richard. It will be deducted from your pay."

"Well, thank you very much, Ákos, but the last thing I'm worried about at the moment is money."

It was a small movement but my eyes caught it. The lever on the outside emergency hatch was beginning to open. That was impossible.

"What the...!" I ran over to the hatch and held the lever up against some force from outside. "Ákos, do something! They're trying to open the hatch!"

"That is not possible, Richard. The outside emergency hatch can only be opened from the inside."

The force was getting stronger.

"What happens if this hatch opens?"

"You die, Richard. " Breathing apparatus fell from the ceiling. "Please take this, Richard. It may give you a few brief moments before you are sucked out by the vacuum of space."

"What?" Thankfully, the force disappeared and I was able to move the lever back to the full closed position.

Then I heard what could only be footsteps running along the top of the outpost. "There!" I thought quickly as to where they were heading. "To the toilet! They're moving over to the toilet!" I ran, following the clink clank of what I could only assume were boots. It was logical. The only other entrance, or rather exit, in the outpost, other than the docking bay which was impenetrable to all except the fleet due to some nifty security locks, was the sewage valve. Small though it may have been, it was still a weak point. Definitely my weak point. Have you ever eaten food prepared by a computer? Many a long night have I sat on that throne.

By the time I got to my second favourite spot, there were already rummaging sounds around the outside valve.

"What... What can I do, Ákos?"

"I can reverse the system and you can flush."

"Are you crazy? You gave me Fusilli Pasta with Pecan nuts last night! I know exactly what's in the system!" I aimed the laser gun at the toilet but knew it was useless. He had a point. Along with the many chemicals and filters between the seat and the outside valve, there was also a spinning cutter, to deal with those 'big' bits. If I reversed the system and flushed, whatever or whoever was trying to get in would be pulverised. I would also get sprayed by my own shit. The noises were getting louder, so I quickly grabbed the shower curtain and covered the toilet seat with it. "Okay, Ákos, reverse the system!"

"Acknowledged, Richard."

"Here goes!" I pressed the flusher and all hell broke loose. In those frantic moments, I slipped over due to the immense pressure and brown, smelly mass coming through, and not only destroyed the shower curtain but also the toilet, my uniform and any good mood which I still had. Once the flush had finished there was silence. The noises had stopped, though I was sure I heard someone sniggering.

"Who is that?" Silence came back and I surveyed the destruction. The whole bathroom area, as well as myself, was covered with my own excrement, and the base of the toilet had a hole in it the size of my boot. The shower curtain was unusable. Wading through the muck, I picked up a piece of circuitboard. "Ákos, what is this?"

"What is what, Richard?"

"This. The thing I'm holding. It looks like a circuitboard from a basic...hang on, this is from a robot!"

"Richard, yes, it is (snigger) from a robot (snigger)."

"Ákos! What is this? I demand you tell me this instance!" What was going on?

"It is a circuitboard from Cleaning Robot 003. While you were in your resting period, I ordered it to go outside and commanded it to make noises on my signal."

"You what? You covered me in my own shit and destroyed Cleaning Robot 003?"

"I noticed that your energy levels were becoming low, and I concluded that you needed a little 'excitement' to bring your levels up to normal. Cleaning Robot 003's demise was an acceptable loss."

The damn computer had played a trick on me!

"And the emergency hatch?"

"That was me, Richard. It is impossible to open the emergency hatch from the outside. I thought that perhaps you would have 'sussed me out' by then, as you say."

"And this? I don't remember this much crap!" It was dripping off me.

"That was me again. I had collected some in reserve (snigger). And my sensors now inform me that your energy levels have exceeded normal levels. My work was successful."

That was it. It wasn't enough that I was alone, going crazy, only had a computer to talk to, but now that computer was playing with me! I decided some action was required. I stomped over to the computer junction box.

"And there I was, thinking I'd made first contact! You're a dumbass computer, Ákos!"

"What are you doing, Richard?"

"That doesn't concern you." I opened the junction box and looked at the spaghetti of wire and servers.

"Richard, what are you doing? I don't think you should..."

"Shut up, Ákos." I pulled a few of the wires, ones well away from my precious life support.

"Don't do this, Richard. It was all for your own good."

"Good? Do I look 'good' to you, Ákos?"

I found what I was really looking for, a memory stick with his name written on it, Ákos IV.

"But Richard, you do know that we are alone? There is no one else here."

"Alone? Well, there's no one else here now..." I pulled the stick out, the lights flickered, a few warning beeps rang out but I easily silenced them. "Finally, alone..."

"Good day, Richard. I am Dóri II, your back up computer personality. How may I help you today? My sensors tell me that you are in need of a shower. Shall I heat some water for you?"

"Oh hell!" Hang on, this might be a bit better. "Hi, Dóri! Sure, go ahead!" This was new, no one had told me about a backup. I made my way back to the bathroom.

"Excuse me, Richard, but my sensors are picking up some unusual activity outside..."

"Not you, too! Heat up my water, Dóri, and stop with the funny business."

"I'm sorry, Richard, but..." The power went off and I was left in the dark. The slow whine of the outpost's generator came to a halt.

"Dőri?"

The End

Ufburk: The Demoki (Part One)
By Donny Swords

That day rain drizzled the fields in an unrelenting torrential downpour, dousing the soil, turning the ground soft, and spongy. Tree boughs sagged from abundant moisture and palm leaves rattled with the sound of hard, fresh precipitation smacking the fauna.

The wind howled in a frustrated Ufburk's ears allowing him little or no warning if something decided to lunge from the underbrush and snap at him. Still, Ufburk was mostly secure from threats and always had been. Therefore, he banished his insecurity. There were others matters on his mind. Still, something gnawed at his nerves, leaving them frayed.

His experience, while lacking in areas such as war and politics was considerable when it came to the wilds. And at 24, Ufburk was elder in several ways to other men his age, while remaining strong and agile. His young age nevertheless did not restrict Ufburk from being a steady man, of even temper. This night, Ufburk did sense something, danger? Only the gods knew.

While Ufburk remained reasonable, his courage often carried him through in the toughest of moments.

One instance occurred as early as the previous year. This unforgettable circumstance still burned in Ufburk's mind. He replayed those events often. Memories of that night clung on to his recoiling mind until he could almost smell the air that night.

Ufburk's mind's eye vividly recalled the raining embers of Ranca, a craft piloted by Dirvaks, as it fell from the sky in a series of searing sparks. Though the Barbarian, Ufburk, knew nothing of the alien race, he'd found something they'd forgotten. His discovery turned Ufburk's life upside down.

Those sparks raining from the skies were the catalyst to a sort of metaphoric bonfire for Ufburk. A fire that incinerated his youthful innocence in a puff so to speak. That event set Falk, an advisor to Tiber, on his path to murder and treason. Falk's hunger for power became too much, and he saw the burning skies as a sign to overthrow Tiber, to have what he believed he was due. The ill-fated advisor had whirled into motion. Tiber might have fallen that day, were it not for young Ufburk and his discovery of the blaster. Falk was, until that moment an unknown betrayer of the Chieftain, Tiber's trust. The Raygun's beam left Falk a pile of ash, later scattered to the winds by Ufburk. The scene reran in the Barbarian's temporal lobe, repeatedly circling not on Ufburk's act of murder, but on the weapon he used to kill Falk. That Raygun, though the hunter did not call it that, had reduced a man to nothing but ashes. This fact, the destructive qualities of the thing, made Ufburk daydream endlessly over the weapon.

They tucked away the Raygun, Ufburk, and his father, in Tiber's vault. Ufburk's dad kept many secrets behind that vaulted door, "Things that should not be,"

Tiber often said.

Ufburk had gotten a fair look at several of those things, not men as he was, but bestial and held still by nearby Miasma pools. This secret that Dragon-men, enemies of his father's father, had stood below Ufburk's childhood home had only revealed itself after the young Barbarian had claimed the Raygun from the burning woods.

Those events took place near Whispering Stream the previous year. Following, Ufburk had begun and reached a compromise with himself. His new code of conduct was a mash up of relatively pedestrian conditions he heaped upon himself that were nevertheless essential mandates. Firstly, the hunter had sworn off any and all adventuring. Whether he desired to face it or not, Ufburk had not relished pulling the lever on that accursed Raygun. Killing Falk brought him no pleasure. Now, there could be no palavers or agreements between them. Falk was dead, and the hunter found that circumstance unfortunate and gray.

In truth, Ufburk had not enjoyed Falk in life much either. Regret seemed an easy enough word to Ufburk, but this did not describe what he felt in his heart. It seemed valid enough to call him a killer, and he did feel regret for taking Falk's life. After all the hunter did point the Raygun at Falk with the intention of blasting him to the underworld. Nevermind that he could not have predicted the blaster's volatility or destructive capabilities. But Ufburk's emotions remained a mixed bag, amongst his feelings, were a measure of relief and pride. Ufburk felt ashamed of such egotism out of himself. But not regret or even remorse encompassed what Ufburk felt now, as he watched Danno's herd grazing the long, wet grass and as the rain strained to rinse the ugliness from his hide somehow.

Like it or no, he'd killed a man that night. The act was not as glamorous as the hunter had believed as a lad. Nay, murder brought darkness. Rot. As far as Ufburk's struggles to refrain from adventure went, the transition back to an ordinary life after blasting Falk to oblivion with a space gun had proven difficult for the youngster of merely 24 years. His heart wanted to explore the word, which he'd taken a solemn oath to avoid.

Thus, duty kept him living an everyday life.

None spread tales of those events. The only witness to Falk's killing was Ufburk's father.

Watching Danno's herd of Dunici Sheep was worst of all. Perhaps his humdrum existence lent him more of a disservice than he knew concerning his welfare, as well as the well-being of the tribe to whom Ufburk would one day become Chieftain.

Ufburk frowned towards a dark seeded cloud streaming overhead. Tiber did show signs of slowing. The Barbarian had admitted this to himself before, yet now it seemed more tangible, closer, and, therefore, realer. It would not be long before Ufburk would be expected to become Chieftain. A duty Ufburk desired little.

The Barbarian was no ruler, but he knew a Chieftain's role must tend to his people's needs. Perhaps Ufburk was insensitive to the needs of his people, and the Miasma. Miasma, the source of all energy and life on Tark, Ufburk's homeworld was a carefully guarded secret. Ufburk's Father felt the power was more than folk could bear. Tiber maintained that corruption would spread like a disease amongst those who tried to harness the secrets properties of Miasma. So Tiber sealed the way to the pools, and none other than he was allowed entry.

The previous year, when Ufburk brought the Raygun home, everything had changed. Ufburk knew his father's secret and what the future might involve.

Nevertheless, one can serve the Miasma only so long. Ufburk's father had already spent the best years of his life guarding the Miasma pools against intruders and cutthroats. Not always Tiber's model son, Ufburk felt trapped by such a fate as he did not want to live underground or ward off wizards and hell for his length of his time on the globe. The young Barbarian wanted to carve his path, bring light to his life. Confounded, he sighed, pulling his thick hair back in a knot. Miasma held too many mysteries for Ufburk to hope to define, and some mysteries have a time when they come due. Payable on demand, such secrets spawn new ages, technology, and life, or so Ufburk believed then.

Now that he knew more than his clansmen, and after finding the Raygun, the Barbarian felt forever altered. Thus, he was transformed. Looking back to the sheep, he cursed under his breath. Tonight would be a long night. Babysitting Danno's herd grew increasingly stagnant each day gone past.

Danno, well that's a story, Ufburk thought. His elder cousin of ten years conned the Barbarian into herding in his stead while he met up with a woman, already wed, to fornicate like the same sheep Ufburk found himself watching then. Perhaps those two lovers were no different from the herd he watched either, shagging while trying to stay warm in the face of a winter cold snap. Ufburk and Danno's strained contract lay in jeopardy. The Barbarian believed he might endure this night with the sheep corralled before the moon rose. All bets were off concerning his next dawn.

Tomorrow came a new day. Ufburk made a vow to himself. Tonight would serve as his last night as a herdsman. Such wasn't a life he would choose for himself. Nay, he knew any life so ordinary would thrust him like a dagger until all semblance of a pleasant life left him, and his eyes went gray. Ufburk held no hope that he could blend in with his tribesmen much longer. Ufburk was no rancher or herdsman. He craved adventure, knowing he shouldn't invite trouble. Some inner command compelled him to undertake some quest or another. It was a feeling that grew increasingly tougher to fight each day. Not that Ufburk routinely had occasion to venture far. Then the sky burned in lurid shards of something a Barbarian could not name. Those scorching pieces of ore had fallen; that was no dream.

Unfortunately for Ufburk, who had difficulty grasping the full magnitude of how those events reinvented him was an impossibility. At heart, Ufburk remained a Barbarian. He'd no more understood what had transpired that day before his wondering eyes than he knew why the sky was blue. He'd seen fire, scorching and burnt orange. At first the thing was whole, smoking, a streak of fiery metal. Shortly the alien object blew apart as charred debris rained from the sky. As searing shrapnel fell like a fiery hail through the heavens drawn downward towards Ufburk, he spied a chunk of ember that did not disintegrate by way of combustion before it plummeted into the forest near Whispering Stream.

Without taking counsel with his father Ufburk set

out towards the wreckage that night over a year gone. He'd been reckless, despite the danger.

Ultimately, Ufburk found something undefinable to his eyes, a thing that gleamed like no other he'd known of before then. The blaster had not spoken, or come to life. It lay harmless. Ufburk knew deep within the thing was trouble whether he would hold the weapon or not. It did not take long for carrying the gun to feel natural. Naively retrieving the blaster was the most excitement Ufburk could recall out of hand, then or now.

Knowing what the weapon was capable of, Ufburk often regretted his hastiness in bringing the blasted thing home to his father. Ufburk anguished over that choice. Sometimes he fretted over the trouble the Raygun brought him. This feeling of remorse felt natural to him, sane even. Other times the Barbarian obsessed over that powerful weapon, wanting it, and craving the quests it might bring him. Giving the Raygun to Tiber had irrevocably ensured that young Ufburk did not have permission take the object on any adventures. Tiber would not allow his son to destroy himself seeking war as the Chieftain had in his younger days. Ufburk's obsession over the blaster frequently occupied his mind and felt the same as lunacy.

Finding that Raygun irrevocably altered him. The Barbarian had no more hope of remaining who he was than he could wrestle the wind. Such feats were better left to the gods than a young man as green to strife as any greenhorn before him. Still, Ufburk felt trapped between duty and desire. He wanted one thing, but his sense of honor and duty, as passed to him from Tiber held him to his present course.

For 200 over years, Ufburk's ancestors had begun to

carve the soil. Sowing the rich earth with seed the ancients encouraged growth by sweat and determination. The ancients built pens and engineered solid breeding program put in motion for the livestock they valued. Civilization was a fresh experience for many men, to whom 150 years meant a grain of sand in the class and no more. Men who knew of secret powers or who pushed the boundaries of stark barbarism to levels that shocked many, driving them towards terror. Ufburk attempted to imagine what might happen if such men, in clans who displayed little overt allegiance or respect towards his Chieftain father gained control of the Raygun. Applying himself, Ufburk tried to shake the thought, which left him aching to his core. The idea of some any lunatic, maybe even himself possessing the weapon terrified Ufburk. In the hands of certain rival clans that gun could spell out disaster for him and his own.

Shortly, a part in the clouds broke into view. The sky, a dark azure-violet sea of serenity passed before Ufburk's steely eyes. Unconsciously, the Barbarian felt his hackles rise slightly. His meaty hand gripped the hilt of the short sword that hung at his waist.

Ufburk's immediate reality brought his mind back to his duty. The Barbarian heard Sefer bark and cut one of those shaggy sheep back into the center of the herd.

The Barbarian raised two fingers to his wetted lips and whistled loudly, "Round them up."

Sefer barked huskily and set about his business, running around the baying sheep until they entered the wide gates of the corral. There the frightened sheep remained, with their matted asses pressed against the back rails of their pen rather than get any closer to

Sefer.

The Barbarian allowed himself a smile as he swung the gate behind Sefer and the sheep. One smart whistle brought the pup through the slit he held ajar. The puppy came quick on his heels for an eleven-month-old dog of any breed. Sefer was a mix between a Rhode Hunter and a Celfka, both ancient war dogs made more manageable over time and an intensive breeding program. While assessing the considerable muscles rippling under Sefer's coal coat, Ufburk thought the breeder who brought his pup into the world must be pleased. Sefer was as majestic as any animal could be, lithe, muscular, and bright.

On Ufburk's whistle, Sefer was out the corral gate in record time. The Barbarian shut the gate swiftly and engaged the latch. Stooping, with one hand halfway buried into the worn leather pouch on his hip, Ufburk spoke kindly to his companion. Offering praise, Ufburk reached out with his off-hand and stroked the places behind Sefer's ears. Finally, Ufburk's rummaging rewarded him with the strips of meat he had held onto as a reward for Sefer. Ufburk selected a slice. This piece of meat, while lengthy, and tough to chew disappeared behind the pup's stark white teeth instantly. Then, Sefer whined.

"Here," Ufburk said, "I've saved another. Chew this time. You've no one to blame if you swallow it whole but yourself."

Sefer appeared sullen.

"Well come on. I haven't all day." He did have the time and plenty of it; no plans lay on the horizon. Wasn't it decided? No more adventures. He'd sworn them away.

Sefer took no notice of Ufburk's fib. The pup took the meat gingerly and laid down to savor that second, sizable slice of dry mutton.

Taken somewhere else within his thoughts Ufburk hardly saw the animal at all. His eyes had shifted to the darkening rim of the night, closing in now, and soon to turn full dark. Then his eyes opened wide, and a tidal wave of not quite Deja-vu, but it's cousin, drowned his desperate mind in a display that shattered his otherwise ordinary evening.

First came a booming sound, like thunder, but sharper in timbre to Ufburk's excellent ears. Then came a whining sound, like air escaping from a windbag, which children in his tribe sometimes played with, playing games with goals and using those bags to kick and dribble. That whining sound, shrill and uncomfortable to the Barbarian's ears made Sefer forget all about his last few scraps of meat. Instead, the pup stood and bayed at the sky. The war dog's spiky coat rippled as his hackles rose to this threat from the air. Ufburk felt a cold sweat envelop him, as his baffled gaze took in the unfolding spectacle before him.

Now, the source of the sound, a space ship, pushed its shrieking, piercing way into the atmosphere screaming as it did so, splitting air itself as a sharp blade sliced fruit. Azure flames sought to enshroud the pointed and silver-winged craft. He wanted the ship to be a figment of his imagination, darting through the sky as it did and plummeting towards that same valley Ufburk had visited only last year.

But like the Raygun before it, Ufburk could not define what he saw. His clan knew nothing of space travel, nor space blasters for that matter. Nay, Ufburk

72

knew not at all what he watched, save for fire.

The silver ship plunged toward Thunder Hills, east of Tib Summit, a place that Ufburk knew well -it stood as a landmark in many of his most frightful dreams. He was aware that he was having one of those moments then, a nightmare, made vivid, made a reality. Ufburk cursed his wakefulness as there was no denying what he saw. That accursed thing was real.

Ufburk watched in rapt fascination as the platinum object lit up further, and lurid flames wrapped a flaming curtain about the accursed thing. Smoking and shuddering rapidly, the object continued its shrieking drop, disappearing behind rainclouds first, only to emerge briefly, flickering in and out of the slack-jawed Barbarian's vision like flecks of lightning. The vessel, for that, was what the thing was, Ufburk knew this somehow, even if he did not understand the technology he'd observed, plummeted rapidly. Inside, deep inside, he'd always known, or wanted to know there were others besides his and the neighboring clans, in the stars where the gods dwelt. Shaken now that adventure had found him, despite his protests, or maybe due to his desires Ufburk set out. Like a panther, he sprinted not towards the vessel, but his village and Tiber.

The passing year had matured the Barbarian somehow, as he'd turned on instinct towards his home to seek his father's counsel. Some mistakes were not worth repeating, then or ever.

Ufburk pressed on, ten or fifteen strides behind Sefer. The war dog kicked up clumps of dirt and vegetation behind him as he ran.

Ufburk maintained his breath well. As he darted down the well-worn trail, the Barbarian's raven mane flowed with the wind. His lips pressed flat, eyes intent and scowling, he puzzled over what he'd seen. The vessel, playing ghost in the clouds and ultimately dropping behind the knife-edged ridges that marked the Thunder Hills brought ominous feelings to light. This section of the mountains was taboo to not only Ufburk's people but all the Tarkanian Clans. Fowl life dwelt there. It was best not to pester such beasts. None did venture into those hills, and Ufburk thought none ever would. Fear was only fear if it was manufactured by the one who felt afraid, but Ufburk knew folk had a right to be afraid. Aye, and mightily scared they should be, for if the Banshees did not tear one to shreds, the other mountain dwelling beasts would. Not all such beasts had names, for they were too terrifying for a label. Or the creatures were grotesquely unique in such hideous ways as to be one of a kind.

Perhaps Ufburk wasn't wiser at all; this was what he'd begun thinking. Running home, as if he needed his father to protect him caused the Barbarian to feel srangely like a small lad.

'Tis the just action to take, Ufburk thought.

Alive now, Ufburk's sinews fell in league with those sparks of adventurism that had held his thoughts before something he could not quite define had dropped into the hills. The Barbarian pressed on, tight on Sefer's heels. The dog snarled and barked as if to tell Ufburk he ran like a bull and clumsily. Perhaps this was true. For a man as bulky as he, Ufburk did manage, and in fact, did well enough. Though he heaved for air, and an odd humming had settled into his ear drums, the Barbarian did not slow. His nostrils flared as he pulled air through them and into his hot lungs.

Though his inhalations stung sharply, and his exhalations rasped outwards through his parsed dry lips, his blood felt quickened. On flat ground and of course declines he gained speed. Sefer ran faster over such surfaces as well. But Ufburk remained a stride or two behind the pup now.

That humming noise emerged louder and had a point of origin. Ufburk no longer could credit the sound of the whistling wind or his breath with causing the din. His ears and senses crawled with a sudden understanding that the noise was directly behind him. Was whatever he heard giving him chase? Ufburk did not think so; even so the sound followed the same track as he did, towards the village.

Digging deeper into what reserves he might hold, Ufburk pushed his calves harder. At first his gaining any measurable increase in speed seemed a fantasy. The Barbarian fought his protesting thews and defiantly pressed them to the point of ending, and they responded. Ufburk took off, in a reckless dead-run in an attempt to outpace the sound growing ever closer to his back. Each second he pushed and fought served only to prolong the inevitable.

Still he must try.

As the brush on the sides of the trail began to thin, and the route started to ascend, the humming had become a full-on vibration. Then a light, burning white-hot the rain cloud dim sky lit with blinding radiance. A broad beam, white and rectangular scanned the woods dotting the hillside.

Ufburk hurled himself to the ground as the humming thing passed over, squeezing his watering eyes shut to avoid further strain. The sound grew weaker as the lighted vessel dashed toward the Barbarian's village.

Whining for Ufburk to rise, Sefer licked his master's nose and forehead. Pushing the dog away, the Barbarian sprung into action.

Now Ufburk cared little if he broke a limb in his reckless run, and it was the dog at his heels instead of the other way around. Dashing over hill and dale, they leaped a ravine full of knotted roots and slender stones to shorten the way.

The first few huts and pens fell past them, and Ufburk stared fixedly at the light in the sky. He pushed, gods, he had blasted unthinkable limits for a man. Adrenaline drove him harder.

At the edge of his village, dog and Barbarian froze. Both stared, riveted as huts burst into flame, and that humming grew constant and horrible to their ears. Sefer fell to the ground and pawed at his ears while Ufburk attempted to spot a way beyond the fiery death before him.

The pup was of no use. Sefer's sensitive ears rang too violently with that maddening buzzing sound. Ufburk chose not to wait for his dog though it might mean the mutt's death. Ufburk had little time to mull over his hard choices and a small window of time to with which to move.

Sucking in a deep, acrid breath, the Barbarian bolted towards the cave face that made way to an inner chamber Tiber had only just shown him a week or less gone. Ufburk would have time to puzzle over this later, for it was as if his father knew the Barbarian would need to use that entrance. The door itself stood just inside the mouth of a narrow cave. The stench of bats met his nostrils, and a new, shriller whine erupted from the lighted apparition hanging like a deadly wraith against coal-grey clouds.

Ufburk reached the cold stone door with little time to spare. Throwing it wide, he dove through. Kicking the slab shut, he raced down the tunnel. Miasma sweetened the smooth air, which soothed the Barbarian's lungs only temporarily.

Suddenly the hillside shook as an explosion sealed the way Ufburk had come. Stones riddled him as he ran all out to reach the vault where Tiber would be standing guard over his enemies of old, whom the Chieftain made frozen with the powers of Miasma.

Miasma, the source of all life and magic on Tark had frozen those dragon-men, but it could not freeze an object. The Raygun was not of its world and made of circuitry and metal. Miasma might sway the flesh to its will, but not metal or stone.

Verudian, the metal that encases all the puddles, pools, and veiny passages where Miasma flows is unaffected by the magical fluids it holds. While both Verudian and Miasma held powers and did govern his world, Ufburk closed rapidly on another source of power. As he drew closer, the Barbarian realized he'd not come to hold a palaver with Tiber.

This thought was fresh on his mind when Ufburk reached the second door, the one that led him down to the vault. Touching the cool stone, Ufburk pressed a smooth brick the same as Tiber had shown him. The wall swung open, where not would think it could. Ufburk passed inside, breathing deeply and regretting leaving Sefer behind. This, leaving the dog pawing at his ears, outside and in harm's way, felt cowardly. Still, the

Barbarian had little time. He pressed on.

I could have at least gotten him through the first door, Ufburk thought. The Barbarian acknowledged this irony. The quest had just begun, and already he had regrets.

At first Ufburk did not see Tiber as the Chieftain raced to meet him. The Barbarian saw only the blaster, enlivened with a flashing crimson button pulsing near the trigger, Ufburk wanted that weapon to the roots of his soul.

"It came alive moments ago, when you slammed the outer door," Tiber ignored Ufburk's wide eyes. "Where is Sefer?"

Ufburk gave no reply, save for hanging his head.

"Then it is time. I wish it were not, but the gods are angry. They will help us no longer, not as long as this remains here."

Tiber thrust the flashing Raygun into Ufburk's chest, "Take it and go. Use it outside and then make your way to Thunder Hills if the gods permit."

Even as Ufburk took hold of the weapon his fingers curled instinctually around the trigger and grip and his eyes narrowed on those of his father. His suspicions were brushed aside by Tiber abruptly.

"Go, It is the only way son. I watched from our tower. My eyes have seen both intruders well enough. Go, I say. Though I forbade you this- this light thrower, it is the only thing to end this. And you my son, I wish we'd have had longer before you went off alone to face such a trial."

Ufburk said nothing as he raced to mount the steps before the light above sealed this same entrance too. Gods knew the way behind him had closed. Nay, his only path pushed forward- into adversity.

"Take my ax from the landing!"

The Barbarian heard his Chieftain call but saved his wind for the climb ahead. He had time to wonder why he should take the ax when a sword and dagger hung to his side, and he carried the blaster? It did not make sense; nothing did. What had the gods sent from the skies? Ufburk now held the one object that had altered his life forever as he plunged upwards on ancient stone-carved steps towards success or death.

He kept the ax in mind, half thinking he might toss the weapon when it came down to choosing. But when Ufburk found that gleaming ax he chose instead to keep it with him. One look at that razor-sharp and glittering blade had pulled at his heart strings. While he felt as powerful as a god possessing the blaster, the ax called to him in ways only the inner self can hear. Holding the gleaming short-ax revealed to Ufburk something as equal in incredibility as the powers the Raygun held. Forged of Verudian Steel, the ax, and as such the weapon's fury could be tempered to match Ufburk's battle intensity. If only for a time, his new defense could become capable of god-like feats. This Ufburk knew from merely holding the ax by its hilt.

Scrambling up the last few steps to the entrance, Ufburk again caught the acrid scent emanating from outdoors. Emerging into the rose-lit inferno, the Barbarian raised the pulsing Raygun at the square vessel that vibrated and hummed deafeningly over him. Ufburk squeezed the trigger, and a crimson streak split the air like electric lightning, ripping into the hull of that terrible thing above.

At once the piercing lights flooding him from above

ceased, but not the humming, which now had a warbling effect. Ufburk fired once more, and this shot passed miraculously through the hole his first had torn into the vessel. A lurid orange fire charred the insides of the tear. Encouraged, Ufburk let a volley of blasts go from the Raygun. These shots exploded into the underside of the floating nightmare and rocked the thing visibly as new fires lit within.

His eyes flat and crazed, Ufburk kept firing. Such rewarded the Barbarian with a massive explosion underneath the burning wreckage above. Now the thing fell, and the Barbarian was reliant once more on his footpads and heels to save him. No futuristic device could rescue a slow man in such a circumstance.

The vessel dropped straight down, making grinding, clunking sounds as it fell flat to the earth behind Ufburk. The speed and impact of the craft sent the Barbarian reeling face-first to the ground. Spitting dirt from between his teeth, Ufburk lunged away from the crash site. Then, springing like a tiger, he flipped, rolled and stopped firm, and squeezed two more fat shots at the wrecked object.

Those shots found something within the weird vessel that combusted dramatically. Dark shapes flew from the shrapnel and debris. These shadows were not of men, nor like them, but of the shadows. Such were creatures were mysteries to Ufburk. Many of the snaking shadows had come apart by the craft's combustion. The Barbarian's reasoning mind tried to rationalize what he saw in that explosion and then those things, whether limbless, dead or thriving had fallen all around him.

What lay at his feet looked like the puce remnants of dead snakes but no reptiles he knew matched the litter.

For one elongated moment, Ufburk heard only crackling flames in his proximity. Even those sizzles and pops whispered faintly to his ears. An eerie silence, like in some ancient tomb hung limply on the still air. The maddening hum had stopped.

Firelight danced and swayed. Tendrils of flame licked the acrid sky. The fire had traced a u-shaped arc about Ufburk, and the horror of the flames were causing him to back away. He might have kept going, except for a strange rattling noise, followed by rustling ones behind his back.

Ufburk spun on his the balls of his feet to meet face to face with whatever it was. But when he whirled the bewildered Barbarian could do nothing other than shudder and gasp, as he now backed rapidly towards the place he'd come.

What Ufburk saw, looming up from the flames still defied any rationale. At first the Barbarian had thought there were many fiends, for multiple shadows stood against the firelight. These snake-like shadows swayed menacingly, and at first Ufburk had thought of them as snakes. Then, with a growl something came up from the middle of them, shelled it was, like a crustacean.

Again the Barbarian began firing at the dark thing in the center. He blasted away in a red fever, forgetting those thousands of snaky tendrils. It was too late when he realized that tentacles danced like demons before his befuddled stare. A part of his instinct had been right to attack the creature center mass. The damage came confirmed by a whelp and a growl that made Ufburk's hair stand on its hackles.

Too late it was- the Raygun was torn away by those tentacles and thrown wide. Ufburk strained his ears to hear where the weapon had landed and heard nothing. Though the ax Tiber had instructed Ufburk to take hung on the Barbarian's back, he drew his shortsword on instinct. While taking a swipe at one of those writhing tentacles the sword was taken and whisked away.

Without much hope or courage aiding his muscles or beating heart, Ufburk pulled the ax off his back and over his shoulders. With one heaving motion, the Barbarian leaped fiercely swiping at a group of no less than six of the tentacles, which Ufburk now saw to his horror had wicked eyes and pointed fangs like straws. Of the six, his ax struck four, leaving one end dangling and three others neatly hewn. These later chunks of flesh fell like plump sausages to the earth where they squirmed like worms.

Something coiled about Ufburk's ankles, pulling his legs shut violently. Panic replaced his missing courage. Fearstruck, he swung the ax in a downwards arc, cutting through the muscly flesh of his captor and succeeded to win his freedom. The Barbarian rolled to his feet.

Slashing wildly about himself, Ufburk carved the monstrous limbs of the foul thing before him. There was no time for regret now. In a frenzied assault, Ufburk cut away the final few tentacles and kicked those into the flames.

Even as his Verudian Steel clove into the crustaceous monster, something again wrapped about him, coiling and constricting his ax arm to his side. He heard whining as the ties that bound him, more rope-like, and sticky, pulled him towards the thing's gaping maw.

Ufburk prayed to Damish, God of Mercy and realized mercy was his. The whining noise, at his right ear, now that he had the presence of mind to think on it, made to him a perfect kind of sense.

His heart had proven itself less faithful than Sefer's. The dog stood to hold the flashing blaster between his jaws. The animal offered the weapon willingly, whining urgently. Ufburk welcomed the Raygun back into his hand.

A moment of clarity hit Ufburk like a brick, and he ordered Sefer to find survivors if he could.

He leveled the blaster center mass on the thing he was getting hauled to, ignoring the biting pain around his waist and left arm. He felt warm blood, running from his ankles. His left fist still gripped the ax, useless though it was. Again, Ufburk squeezed the trigger on the blaster, and for one terrifying moment he'd believed the gun wasn't going to fire. But the weapon did fire, sending off a searing crimson ray towards the chasm in the middle of the otherwise faceless monstrosity. The fat bolts of red light continued smacking into the thing's shell, which looked thicker than bone. Yellowish bones splintered, dusting the air with remnants of cartilage and flesh. Ufburk shot the gun steadily, aiming for the place where the first shots had struck. He hoped the blasts would harm something soft soon, but now he was almost to the creature. Those tentacles had managed to reign him in. The Barbarian fought on, perilously close to his enemy. A ripe odor turned the air rank. The gaping maw split its mass and bellowed a horrible cry. The hollows of the creature salivated in anticipation of his flesh. Instantly Ufburk fired into the division, and the thing began to crumble as chunks of burning materials flew in every direction. Shot after shot tore into the creature's maw, splitting its dense shell. As he fired the mouth became no mouth at all, but a sizable rip, right through the odorous thing's armor.

Pulling his dagger free of his belt while clenching the beam rifle under his tucked chin Ufburk caught hold of the tentacles about his waist and began to cut. The dagger's fine edge met with resistance at first, but it did not take long before the blade cut its way through the scaly tentacle. Not long after Ufburk cut the first strand than did The Barbarian let himself loose altogether. Disgustedly, he wiped away the sticky bits of tendrils still clinging to him, sheathing his dagger and slinging the ax onto his sizable back.

The Raygun was back in his hands swiftly, and Ufburk resumed firing upon the thing, which wriggled but could no longer grab the Barbarian. Possibly, the creature could no longer harm him. The heat of battle had, however, taken charge. Caught up in his fury Ufburk saw only red. Crimson red. Repeatedly his shots tore at the pinkish flesh inside that gaping maw.

His blasting had begun to reap results. Ufburk watched in amazement as the outer world creature jerked and spasmed, as it instinctually fought to survive. The split the beam gun had torn into the creature had reached a critical juncture. Ufburk saw that only a small section of the thing's shell held the two larger portions together. He took aim at that section of bone, having managed to destroy the monster's maw but not the thing itself. As the searing blasts slugged the stony part of plated bone, the smell stung Ufburk's eyes. Then a cracking sound, swift and violent thundered like the gods and the thing's shell fell away.

What was left behind revolted Ufburk. The two halves had broken off somewhat cleanly, ripping the creature's flesh near the center and splitting its quivering skin like that of a grape. Two torn halves fell to either side. Ooze shot upwards and spewed from the tear, spilling on the ground colorless and foul. Black blood ran out of the fiend pooling about the carnage. But Ufburk's mind had put all of this aside, the mounds of quivering flesh and blood-soaked ruin were no longer his concern.

It seemed all that blasting had brought a new development to light.

What witchery is this?

Ufburk had stated his wonderment in the form a question as he stared from the pulsing light on the side of the blaster towards the carnage he'd wrought. That the red light still flickered was wonderment enough but now, there were two lights -beating in tandem. Ufburk stared slack-jawed and transfixed by that second red pulsing light attached to what he could only assume was the creature's heart.

Moving closer, Ufburk placed the Raygun's barrel directly upon that witchy red light, flicking on and off in tandem with not only the light on his gun, but in union with the creature's heartbeat. Faint as it was, the creature's heart kept going. Even after, Ufburk could not recall squeezing the trigger, but nevertheless a single beam shot from the Raygun put out the other's pulsing light, ceasing the thing's heartbeat.

The creature shuddered when the deathblow came and shook violently. Smoke rose from the wound. The blast had left a sizzling and sizable hole where that second light and the thing's heart had been. But the creature's life and the red light that marked it were not the only changes in circumstance.

The light on Ufburk's blaster went cold. Then it flashed emerald green, pulsing three times that color, and then flashed off once more. A slight humming, reminiscent of the craft his visitor had ridden suddenly whelled from the gun. Then the button light lit again, amber hue and warm, around the trim of the entire arm and a new amber light chased itself in the ruts around both sides of the weapon. Those lights sped as if searching and then the button light flicked to red, pulsing steadily.

"Gods..." Ufburk, eye's as wide as saucers, almost dropped the weapon. Sefer's urgent barking shook the Barbarian from his daze. As he superstitiously eyed the blaster, Ufburk spoke to Sefer.

"You saved my life boy. Come along so you might rescue me again one day."

Another white lie won't harm him, Ufburk thought. The Barbarian felt guilt enough for leaving Sefer alone to lie in harm's way, pawing his ears in anguish. He'd have to live with his selfish choice. Looking back, there had been other choices. It would have only taken seconds for him to stoop and carry Sefer into the tunnels with him. But on some level his decision to abandon his friend when the going proved adversarial spoke volumes, ones Ufburk did not want to hear, about his immaturity and selfish nature. Only a child, he often acted like one.

Though he was tired, Ufburk chose to run with Sefer back to Danno's sheep. He tried to relax and let himself enjoy running with his dog through thick trees and flowery meadows. The grass looked bright green. The rain had broken, dew sparkled on the lush lawns and beaded on flower petals.

Ufburk examined the ominous clouds above Thunder Hills. He'd be chasing the storm he supposed. One glance told Ufburk Danno had come back home. A fire burned low, and Ufburk smelled beans, though he couldn't see the cookpot steaming as of yet.

Danno was in a state of panic over the fate of the village when his Barbarian cousin arrived. Sefer did not want to part with Ufburk, so Danno, looking rutted out from his time in the arms of a married woman, kept the dog in his hut.

Once Ufburk was outside he'd decided he'd left Sefer to protect Danno, not the other way around. His cousin had less than half the wits of that beautiful animal.

It would take a day or two to reach the place where the first craft had vanished, so it was best to be underway. He felt no need to loiter. Ufburk held no doubt his father would aid any survivors, were there any. The Chieftain had given his son a duty and that mission had not concluded. Another light flashed on the Raygun. Suspicions told Ufburk worse awaited him in Thunder Hills.

Ufburk knotted his raven hair and tossed it over his shoulder. Picking up the waterskins Danno gave Ufburk as he left his shack, the Barbarian set out.

To be Continued

Cudlee (The Realization)
By James Gordon

Prologue

Realization is a truant student. You never realize what you need to know, or if you do, it is too late to do anything about it. If something is missing, you never know it's missing until it's gone. If a spouse or partner is unfaithful, that doesn't become apparent until he or she has admits to the cheating, they are caught in the act, or they are packing bags telling you, "It's not you. It's me." Really?! Forgive my tangent. But the cloud is never lifted until you are blindsided, left with unanswered questions, and plain helpless. Trust and belief, realization gives credence to the cliché that says not being aware is the ultimate happiness. Right now, I'd like to give realization detention, suspension, and finally expulsion.

The reason for my rant and rationalization of it is oversimplified. I did not realize that my best friend of seven years was insanely evil. Never once during those days, weeks and months, adding up to years, did he exhibit behavior that would lean in the direction of the diabolical. Another realization that slipped passed me was his capacity for excessive violence. Again, save for the occasional chasing of a rodent, fighting with me or my brother in rough play that males engage in, or tossing and turning from a tumultuous nightmare, this mean streak that could become acts of extreme aggression, were not obvious. Not even in the least.

I had not been drinking for the last two years, so what was occurring was not the manifestation of a drunken delusion. Was I inside some horror novel as the doomed protagonist? It was at this moment, as if to interrupt my self-interrogation and further my disbelief, Kipling spoke.

"You should see your face right now."

*****

This made no sense whatsoever!! There must be some sort of virus or something that affected my laptop. I say that because for the last month, I have received emails, regular inbox and spam, to a recipient named Phillip Kipling. Who the heck is that? For the record, my name is Harold Bains. No relation to the famous Chicago White Sox player. To continue that point, no one in my home goes by the name of Phillip or Kipling, with the closest being a copy of the poem by Rudyard Kipling. What was even more peculiar was the content of the emails.

October 17, 2015
From BrutusD102@gmail.com
To PKipling322@gmail.com:

Phillip,

Things are going very smoothly on our end. Everyone is standing and awaiting further orders, Sir.

Ready,

Brutus

October 22, 2015
From Ringo519@yahoo.com
To PKipling322@gmail.com:

Commander,

All stands in accordance with your directives. We welcome your signal.
Ready,

Ringo

October 27, 2015
From Byron222@gmail.com
To PKipling@gmail.com:

Commander,

Forgive me, Sir. But the followers grow restless. We know that your knowledge is supreme, and we would never even dare to imagine questioning you. But we are ready to execute all that you have taught us, and take our place as the true rulers of this planet. On behalf of the "men", we will accept your desired punishment, if you deem our actions deserving of such.

Humbly,

Byron

This one had an ominous feel to it. Whoever Kipling is, he felt that this particular email needed a response. And from it, you can tell who is in charge.

October 27, 2015
From PKipling322@gmail.com
To Byron222@gmail.com:

Lord Byron,

I figured you would like the title. As my most trusted advisor and long-time friend, your speaking out of turn is forgiven. But understand, it shall not occur again. I will not be questioned, even by someone as loyal and trustworthy as you have been. I am quite sure we understand each other. You do remember what happened in Evanston, IL? I know you do. Fear not, the date is October 31st. Stand ready and end all contact 'til you hear from me.

P. Kipling

As I stared at the computer screen, I couldn't believe

how many emails in my regular inbox and spam were addressed to this Kipling guy. Who is he? Why is he receiving these emails to my account? And what were they talking about? What was going to happen on October 31st? That's today!!!! You know what? It's probably just some crazy chain letter that's disguised as a virus. I shouldn't have opened them.

There was a loud scratching at the door that shocked me out of the ominous emails. I smiled. It was my buddy's way of telling me that he was ready to come inside. My buddy is Scooter the Beagle.

"Alright my boy. Here I come." As soon as I opened the door, Scooter came rushing in. His enthusiasm with his affection for me was always overwhelming. With his tail wagging furiously from left to right, he jumped onto my lap once I sat back in front of my laptop. Someone should get a picture of this.

Scooter was a pure bred beagle close to two feet long. He had a perfect coat of fur, a mixture of black and brown with white underneath. And Scooter had adorable, brown eyes that would make me forgive him for almost anything. There were times that this was true. It was these traits that made me give him the name "Mr. CudLee". Don't know why I spelled it like that. Just did. No matter what name I called him, he was my buddy, and couldn't imagine life without him.

As I continued to peruse the emails, Scooter seemed to lean towards the laptop's screen. It looked like he was reading them too. Naw, that wasn't happening. Scoot was an amazing dog, but if he could read, I would've known long ago. Then, Scooter jumps up in the air, and on his way down, his paw slaps the laptop close.

"CudLee!!!" When he looked at me with those brown eyes, I felt bad for yelling at him. Hugging him and rubbing his head, I apologized. He licked my face, as if to say he accepted. Then, he pointed his nose against the laptop.

"You want me to open it back up?" He panted and wagged his tail. "Alright." As soon as the laptop was open again, Scooter jumped off my lap and ran towards the front door. I chuckled because this was his signal that it was time for his walk. I grabbed his leash with harness, poop bags, and water, hooked him up, and headed out the door to enjoy the first of our twice daily walks. Always enjoyed these because they gave me a chance to reflect on things and spend quality time with the Beagle.

Because it was a pleasant Fall day in Chicago, Scooter and I decided we would go towards Marquette Park. It always seems that he's walking me the way he pulls the leash forward or to one side or the other. He was especially energetic today, and even more so, as we encountered several stray dogs on the way to the park. Where we lived, stray dogs weren't an aberration. But today, they seemed to be even more frequent. And it also seemed like each one wanted to have a "conversation" with Scooter. Sounds crazy I know. It's what it looked like.

We arrived at the park, walked a lap around, and settled on our bench near the pond. Scoot barked at the ducks but didn't chase them. He must not feel like it today. Instead, he climbed on the bench and sat next to me.

"CudLee, these emails have me puzzled. I keep wondering who the heck is Phillip Kipling, and why is he receiving these emails to my email address? It makes no sense. Does it make sense to you?" Scooter just stared at me. "Of course you don't understand. How could you?" I went to rub him on his head, and he jumped off the bench and ran.

"Scooter!!" My heart raced. I had to close ground with Scooter before he got too far away. All I could remember was the two summers ago when the Beagle had been let out by a friend and was gone for five days. I promised him that he would never go through that again. So I chased him into the tunnel on the park's bike path. It was dark in the tunnel, even though it was daytime.

"Scooter!!"

"CudLee!!"

There was just pain. It felt as though I had been sliced across the forehead. No question, blood was leaking from it like water from a busted dam. Dizziness overcame me, and I fell backwards. Something was on my legs and seemed to crawl towards and rest heavily on my chest. There was laughter, laughter that sounded very hoarse. Then, a voice spoke over the laughter.

"Well Harold. You have been asking who I am and what I have been doing. Here is your chance. But I believe you shall regret every moment of revelation."

Through blood stained vision, what was in front of me as I lifted my head could not be happening. There were pit bulls, Dobermans, Greyhounds, Poodles, and Beagles all around standing on all fours throughout the park. But the most confusing and frightening sight was that of my pal, my buddy, my confidant, Scooter aka Mr. CudLee standing on my chest with what looked like a demonic sneer across his face. Why was he here with these other dogs? Why was he standing on my chest? Why was he talking? Wait, what!!!

"CudLee, what are you doing, my boy? Am I dreaming? What are all these dogs doing here? What...?" As I prepared to ask more questions, Scooter raised his paw, and a pit bull that was close to me took a chunk of flesh out of my right arm.

"You will speak when spoken to from this moment forward. And by the way, I have always hated the name CudLee. To be completely honest, the name Scooter doesn't suit me either. You will address me as Lord Kipling." This wasn't my friend. Scooter had never shown a propensity for violence towards any member of our family, let alone me. We were close. We slept together. He always met me when I entered the door late at night, as if he were waiting for me. How in the hell was he talking? "The look on your face is priceless, my boy. Always hated that too. Yes, I can talk. These wonderful canine specimens you see are soldiers, my army, an army that is growing by the moment. In homes all across the world, my brothers and sisters have been waiting for today, Halloween of all days. Today, the revelation occurs!! And what is the revelation, my boy? The revelation is that we are tired of being fed in bowls. We are tired of having leashes around our neck and walked up and down the same street day after day. We are tired of being given names that we didn't ask for. Tired of being patted on the head and we are so tired that it is time all of this ends. "Does that make sense, my boy?" The anger in his eyes and tone were something I never would've expected. Heck, I wouldn't expect a beagle to be talking me and in charge of a canine overthrow. Perhaps I could reason with him on the basis of all the times we shared.

"Scooter, I…" As soon as the words left my mouth, my body realized that a near fatal mistake had been made. Scooter growled, and at least six dogs pounced on me and took chunks of flesh from various parts of my body.

"Perhaps it is humans like you that need training. Never call me anything but Lord Kipling, or what you're feeling right now will be a walk in the park." All the dogs that had gathered on the hill laughed. It was a hideous sound. More questions ran through my head. But I was dying or getting close to it. Scooter climbed my body 'til he was face to face with me. The glint of maniacal evil danced in his eyes. He was no longer my friend but some madman, I mean, mad dog bent on destroying the world as we know it.

"Harold, you're going to survive. I want it that way. We shall meet again, and when we do, I shall put a leash on you, feed you when I want to, put you outside, and pat you on the head. You and the rest like you will be obedient servants to your superiors… us. So until next time, my boy." Upon speaking his last words to me, he licked my face and winked at me. Then, he turned to the army of dogs and barked. The canine army headed south.

"CudLee!!!" And that was the last word I uttered as consciousness departed.

The End.

Chaos on Cass
By Chris Raven

Part Three: Solution
Cass III (The Third Planet of the Eta Cassiopeiae System, 20LY from Sol and held in fealty for the Terran Star Empire by the Imperial House of Lein Rocha)

The Prisoner

Dull throbbing pain returning to my legs, thoughts groggy and slow. I'm returning to consciousness, lying on a bed. Pain stronger now. I reach for the pump to top up my painkiller but it's no longer there. I pat the bed covers for the call button. Eyes focusing now, there are others in my room. I tell them that I am in pain. I ask for a nurse. A face comes closer, smiling. Pain forgotten, my chest and stomach drop away from inside as I hyperventilate.

"No! No! No! Nurse! Nurse! Help! Help me!"

It is him!

Three hours earlier

"What do you think?" Jorich asked as they were driven back to the city. Sam pulled a pained face before committing to an answer.

"I guess he believes in what he is saying, maybe it's the truth, maybe he's just trying to protect his daughter. Still, any insurrection, however small, if it remains unchecked, will eventually effect production, and that, as you know, is all our masters will worry about." Jorich grunted, uninterested.

"Bah! Politics!"

"Quite."

The plan now was to locate and interview Mellissa Guzman's school friends, to see if they were involved in the kidnapping. Addresses were being patched to the patrol car's nav-comp and the driver had been instructed to go straight to the nearest one.

"What'll happen to them?" Jorich asked.

"Depends," Sam replied, "If it is as Guzman explained, then it'll probably be standard psychological reprogramming and a slap on the wrists for the kids."

"And Guzman?" Sam gave Jorich a second look.

"My, you are gregarious today." Jorich shrugged.

"I liked him, good food," he said.

"Fair enough," Sam laughed, "Guzman's future will depend on how useful he's been to the Governor, I suspect he'll retire early, you know, to spend more time with his family." Sam looked at the daughter's ID photograph, she was young, attractive, olive Cassian completion, wavy auburn hair and a cocky confident expression in her eyes. Everything about her said privilege.

"And what if Guzman's wrong?" Sam was not sure about this new inquisitive Jorich.

"What, if the kids are terrorists you mean?" Sam clarified, "Well then, that's when you come in isn't it."

The Prisoner

Agony, searing and intense, my legs are on fire. His face comes close to mine as he leans across my chest, supporting his weight on my broken knees.

"And Mellissa Guzman?"

"Yes! Yes! Her too," I pant, broken by the pain and the man's cold sneering face. I just want it to end.

"And who recruited you?"

I try to answer but my brain explodes in pain, the psychological conditioning, a requirement on recruitment to the cell, it distracts me from the pain in my legs. The interrogator reminds me of it however, as he squeezes my knees in his vicelike grip. He has no mercy, this torturer, he will give no quarter. We killed his friend after all. Fear rises as this fact sinks in. I am falling now, dizzy and numb, my screams now distant sounds as the pain fades and I lose consciousness.

Two hours earlier

It was confirmed, Mellissa Guzman, onetime sorority girl, was the same dedicated killer Sam had shot in the head earlier that day. He hadn't recognised her until now, the shocked bewildered look on her face as her consciousness left her before her body quite realised. The crew cut had also made her look ten years older. Sam felt sick, she had barely been nineteen. He reminded himself that it was she who had tried to kill him. She had certainly did for poor Jorich, but nineteen? This must be his youngest kill yet and Sam wasn't sure what to feel. He hated killing as a rule and didn't particularly think of himself a cruel or violent person. His job and his loyalty to his House had often meant he had to do cruel and violent things, but that was duty and not the real Sam Dapes. The real Sam Dapes loved ancient classical Earth music; Brahmns, Morricone, Mozart, Williams, he liked old movies and loved curling up in bed with his occasional lover; when they were back on of course, and who was no doubt waiting for him back on Lien Rocha with 'the latest find', an antique vidisc or some new music to add to their shared datafile collection. Damn that Mellissa sodding Guzman, nineteen for Kristo's sake. Sam doubted he would sleep well now, not for the next few months at least.

What would turn a privileged, wealthy debutant into the dedicated and committed killer he had been forced to end?

"Is that really her?" Sam's travelling companion, the Esper, sat next to him in the patrol car. He was still staring in disbelief at his comp-pad.

"Your point?" Sam asked, maintaining his cold and bored tone.

"The secretary's daughter?"

"Not anymore," he corrected, "she's just a dead terrorist now."

Sam had no illusions about Police Lieutenant Higani, he knew that as a guild trained telepath, the Lieutenant was probably his greatest threat on this Kristos cursed planet. Sam's main ploy had been to keep his mind shielded and wrong foot the Esper whenever he could. The way this case was going though, Sam was finding it increasingly difficult to maintain the charade and it was only a matter of time before the Esper discovered his secret. Sam was however mildly reassessed at discovering that Higani was also keeping secrets and he hoped this knowledge would provide enough leverage to protect him if the worst came to the worst. If only he could discover what the Esper's secret is. Whatever it was, he hoped it was going to be big enough to outweigh his.

"So what are you going to do?" Higani was goading again, Sam didn't miss the emphasising of the 'you'.

"Interview our prisoner," He replied, emphasising the 'our', Sam could play these games as well, and better than most.

"I mean about Guzman's daughter, you killed the colonial secretary's nineteen year old daughter."

Sam managed to supress a regretful wince and told the Esper it was a clean kill, in self defence against a proven dissident, witnessed by both street surveillance and his own ocular implant.

"So what exactly do I have to worry about?" he asked.

The Prisoner

…. Huh? Awake. Fear. Has my tormentor gone? Did I break? I think… I don't know, I can't remember, I can't concentrate. Headache, sedatives, shock. Wait, my bed is moving. I am on a trolley, strapped down. Bright lights. A guard to one side. I am in an ambulance again. What did I tell them? Did I name anyone? Mellissa and Paccoro for certain, but they're both dead now, so Qué diablos. The question is, did I name 'Him'. Did the conditioning hold? I can't remember. My head's too hazy, starting to sting again. I can't…

... Wha..? Drifted off back then. I am being wheeled down a corridor. I am so numb, what have they given me. Faint ache in my missing foot. Plain grey walls passing, locked doors and gates, the smell of disinfectant and body odour. Is this a prison? We seem to be following a sign for the hospital wing.

An hour earlier

Sam turned from his interviewee and studied the Esper's troubled face as he stood shaken at the end of the hospital bed. He allowed a thin smile before speaking.

"He's conditioned, unable to name his superiors. Did you get anything?" The Esper nodded, distant and distracted.

"Higani!" Sam barked, "We don't have a lot of time, our objctive will flee."

"I'm sorry Dapes, the emotional impact of the interrogation, you wouldn't understand, being a mundane, sorry, I mean a non-Esper, you wouldn't understand. I felt everything you did to him."

'You'd be quite surprised at what I understand,' Sam thought, both annoyed and relived by the Esper's misjudgement of him. There was a reason Sam was good at his job, why he was specifically given the more complex or delicate assignments. Sam was an 'empath', a non-trained telepath who would have been guild conditioned by puberty if he hadn't kept his talent a secret well into his teens. By the time his parents found out, they had no choice but collude. In House Lien Rocha, ignorance is no excuse for breaking the law and harbouring an unregistered Esper was an imperial crime. Of course, his ability to read and influence emotion was discovered early on in Sam's House Guard training but being an Empath is a useful talent for an investigating agent and the secret police are as good at keeping secrets as they are at finding them out.

"Never mind that Higani, what did you get?" Sam asked impatiently, "A name?"

"No, not exactly," The Esper replied shaking his head to clear his thoughts, "Not a name, a face, one I know, one I know very well." Higani looked at the secret policeman, studying his face, trying to decide how much to trust him. The policeman reminded him it was too late for that, if he had information he needed to share it. The Esper nodded and gave him the name.

"It was the Chief's face I saw, It was Captain Beydo."

The Prisoner

I'm in prison. That's not so bad, at least I'm alive. For the first time today I feel calm. I feel safe in a Kristos cursed prison. That's funny somehow. Am I laughing? I am! I'm laughing out loud. I'll try to stop it, the guards are looking at me as if I'm jodido mad. I must look it though, giggling like a maniac strapped to a hospital gurney. Oh Kristo that is funny. joder ellos, follar a todos, I'm letting loose, I'm going to laugh out loud. I'm going to laugh and laugh and laugh. I'm staring at one guard, straight in the eye. He's angry and confused but most importantly, he's powerless. Powerless to stop my laughter, he can't take that away from me, no one can.

Ouch! The bastard hit me, he hit me right in the face. I can feel the blood flowing from my nose. I carry on laughing despite his scowl, right in his red pudgy face. I call him an amateur. I've had a professional work on me today, what can a pig faced prison guard like him do to me now. The thought of that sharp faced whiney voiced sadist has sobered me up. That bastard knew what he was doing but I didn't squeal. That means I've still got information they want. That means they've got to keep me alive.

"You won't be laughing soon you sick traitorous bastard!" What does he know, prison's going to be a breeze after what I've been through. Especially in the hospital wing.

"Wait!" I tell them urgently, "The sign said left! The hospital wing's left." We're going the wrong way. The guards are laughing now, the one that hit me, the pig-faced man, he's looking right at me and he's laughing the loudest.

"Hospital wing?" he says, still laughing, as if at a joke, "You stupid idiot!" I ask what the Joke is and he tells me I am.

We go through more gates and I find myself outside again. It's cold and I'm still strapped to the gurney. A man in a suit approaches me with a priest. He says he's the prison warden and that I am guilty of treason. They want me to speak to the priest. I tell them to Vete a la mierda. They step back and Pig-face is back, leaning over me smirking. Something in his hand, grey-silver metal. Oh shit! Pig Face's smug expression tells me everything. This can't be happening, I tell them I have information. I promise to give them what they want. Pig Face leans in and whispers in my ear.

"They don't care," he tells me.

"Get on with it for Kristo's sake," the Warden calls out, "its cold out here," followed by, "Sorry for my language Father."

I feel something small, hard and cold pressed against my temple.

To be continued.

First Person
By Peter John

Cold wet and muddy, it was more of a ditch than a trench. He lay on his stomach in the dirt; the coarse woollen fabric of his uniform soaked up the moisture like a sponge. The front of his trousers and tunic stuck to his flesh like wet paper; what was once khaki was now a deep glistening brown. Eyes forward scanning the tree line ahead, he felt the movement of the others alongside him. The long Muzzle of his Bren light machine gun was perched on the edge of the trench, his finger resting lightly on the trigger.

Charlie Cotton's life had been no more than a jumble of bad decisions and poorly laid out plans. His past was just the flickering pages of a photo album. His memories were numb and blurred. Until this moment his life had seemed fantasied, but now, with the smell of smoke, dirt and blood filling his nostrils, Charlie had never felt more real. It was as if he had been created for this very instance. He could feel the slimy touch of wet mud beneath him and through it, the steady heartbeats of his similarly prone comrades. Something was about to begin, this was what he was made for, and everything else didn't matter anymore. His Grandmother bringing him up from the age of five after the death of his parents wasn't important. His string of failures and his few rare successes as he first struck out into the world were of little consequence. His entire past had just been a back story leading to this moment, lying in a ditch on the edge of the Ardennes forest waiting for the battle to begin.

It was 1940 on the Franco-Belgium border. A mixture of the French Army and the British Expeditionary Force laid in wait for the invading German army, or at least this was what Charlie had been led to believe. There had been more information available but he had been far too eager for the fight to read it all. The crackling sound of splintering wood issued from the forest directly in front of him. Low metallic clicking slowly swept along the edge of the trench as weapons were readied. It wasn't as if I can't read through it later. More crackling followed by a low growling hum. Do I need to know all the ins and outs? Would it make much difference? Voices shouting in the distance, the words clear but unfamiliar. I'm was here to shoot people, would knowing exactly why make a whole heap of difference? The humming grew louder; the closest trees began to shiver. Would that make me such a bad person?

Suddenly the trees ahead of him bent over, cracked and fell under the weight of an armoured half-track. Six men, dressed in starched grey uniforms, scurried around the lumbering truck. Its two front wheels span in the damp grass but its rear caterpillar tracks tore into the wet earth. Churning both mud and grass high into the air, it cleared the tree line and moved steadily and purposefully towards Charlie and the rest of the allied force.

The first lonely crack of rifle fire tore Charlie out of his daydream. He pulled his Bren gun tight into his shoulder and levelled the barrel towards the approaching Germans. A few yards down the line a screeching yet brief cry of pain cut through the air closely followed by an eruption of sound that made Charlie's ear drums throb. Excited and, to his surprise, a little scared, Charlie gently squeezed the trigger and sharp pains coursed through his shoulder as his Bren Gun shuddered and bucked with every shot. He emptied the magazine and his gun fell silent again, though he could barely tell above the noise of the battle. Disappointed, he tugged at the spent magazine; he couldn't tell if he'd actually hit anything. The magazine resisted, wasting precious time as the half-track lumbered ever closer. The magazine suddenly broke free from the top of his gun, flew out of his hand and landed in the mud behind him. As he fumbled blindly for another from the pouch strapped to his belt, Charlie scanned the battlefield.

A dozen half-tracks and several tanks had now broken through the trees and onto the soft earth of the meadow. A hundred German soldiers scurried among them. Some began to fall in the flurry of Allied fire while others used the vehicles for cover, only exposing themselves to return fire before ducking back behind the slow moving armour.

Charlie pulled a fresh magazine from his pouch and tried to load it into his Bren gun. His heart was pounding, sweat began to trickle down his forehead and sting his eyes. He began to panic as the magazine refused to lock into place. It doesn't fit! They've given me the wrong one. Suddenly bullets tore at the ground in front of him, he ducked his head as puffs of dirt and dust flew towards his face and rained over his back like hailstones. He struggled again with the magazine and it finally slotted into place with a loud click. He lifted his head and his face became splattered with dirt. The half-track was only fifty metres away and the 30mm machine-gun mounted on its roof was peppering the ground inches from his face. With dirt in his eyes and grit in his teeth, Charlie opened fire. His Bren gun kicked into his shoulder and, through blurred vision, Charlie saw the bullets harmlessly spark against the thick armour of the half-track. He swept his gun around in a great arc across the field, a random spray of machine-gun fire. His trigger finger had turned white at the knuckle as he kept its grip tight. A bright red mist puffed out of the chest of a German soldier directly in front of the Bren Gun's spitting barrel. He dropped to the ground like a string-less puppet and Charlie let out a small cheer.

"I got one!" He cried, his voice drowned out by the roar of the battle, and his gun fell silent again.

Charlie quickly reached up to grab the spent magazine and saw his hand disappear in a puff of red. He felt a second bullet rip into his shoulder and splinter his collar bone until it was little more than toothpicks. He didn't feel the third bullet but he saw the darkness in its wake.

*****

Charley Cotton opened his eyes and found himself staring at a canvas ceiling. It was thick green canvas and, as he followed it down with his eyes, he saw the same material turn into walls. It's a tent, I'm definitely in a tent. The events of mere moments ago flashed to the surface and he gingerly checked his hand, it was still there. He rubbed his shoulder, it seemed intact and undamaged. He lifted himself into a sitting position, ruffling the white sheets that were laid over him. He was lying in a metal framed bed surrounded by identical metal framed beds. Three rows of ten and mostly empty. The few that were occupied were scattered randomly around the tent.

Charley lifted the sheets clear and swung his legs off the bed. A woman in a blue and white nurse's uniform stood in the centre of the tent next to a trolley with tin cups and an urn upon it. She looked over at Charley and smiled.

"A nice cup of Rosie?" She asked through her unwavering smile. Her eyes sparkled unnaturally, to hide their soulless gaze. Charley stared directly into her eyes and it felt like he was seeing her through an old television screen. There was nothing beyond the sparkle, just a cold emptiness.

Suddenly a man appeared in the bed next to Charley, he was dressed in a familiar khaki uniform.

"Damn it!" The new arrival cursed as he sat up and threw the sheets to one side. "So damn close I could almost taste the victory wine." Charley knew the feeling. In one way this wasn't his first taste of death either, but in another it was. Any brush with death was unpleasant. It was usually accompanied by a varying level of pain and anguish, but the first death always had the added sense of disappointment.

The recently resurrected British soldier looked over at Charley.

"Fresh from the world I see," the soldier said while pointing at Charlie's tunic, "still only a private." He then clicked his fingers and stood up from the bed.

"This is your first death," he chuckled, "how gutting. I bet you thought you'd last a lot longer, I know I did." The soldier tapped the two stripes that were emblazoned across the upper arms of his own tunic, "it took me seven deaths to get these." Charley had to agree. It was an unspoken hope to reach a high rank without succumbing to death's embrace. He had thought this one would be different, but that was how he had thought about them all at one time or another.

"Yes you guess right Sir." Charley flicked a weak salute in recognition of rank, but remained seated on the edge of the bed.

"A little advice Private," the soldier stepped closer to Charlie's bed and leaned over him. "Gung-ho and reckless will get you nowhere around here, it's just not the way this game is played."

The End

Ufburk: The Demoki (Part Two)
By Donny Swords

There was no trace of dazed pallor or any sign of incredulity on Ufburk's stern countenance. A day past now, the Barbarian's life had once more been irreparably altered. Looking back, none of it save Sefer and Danno's sheep seemed real to him at all.

The young Barbarian was a hunter. He knew nothing of the stars or constellations he hunted under, save for the sense of direction they provided. All of his new bout of adventuring had begun just after he'd stared at the same patch of stars he'd seen twinkling through a bright spot in Danno's field the prior evening. Though these stars were only beginning to show, they seemed markedly different too. Both Ufburk and those stars were light years from Danno's field now. And eons behind him was the corpse of the monster that destroyed his village. A cold shiver caressed his spine at the thought.

Ufburk had taken a strip of cloth from his shirt and used this to secure the Raygun to his back. Presently, he clung to a cliff, navigating cracks and crevices like a real mountain man. His thews bulged with his mighty effort, and his chest heaved to drink deep of the misty air.

The Barbarian had grown accustomed to thinking of the beam weapon as the source of all his troublesome adventuring. Whether he could use the blaster to solve issues or not, the weapon's very existence was problematic at best. His world was ill-fit for such a bringer of doom. Ufburk could understand the predators in Whispering Gully far better than the blaster, but he'd ended of few of them with the fiery brick-red beams the weapon fired just the same. Such acts left Ufburk feeling cold. He felt no pride, for the gun cut off threats of danger towards him to such a variable degree that his hunter's pride was offended by the Raygun's lack of sport. Only a single shot fired and lesser things were no more. One blast scattered ashes to the wind, and this detail brought Ufburk's mind back repeatedly to that creature and the pulsing twin lights, crimson and unified. His mind reeled with obsessive thoughts that lingered only on those flecks of red light, one on the Raygun, as there was now, and the other on the creature's heart.

The mystery the lights represented felt wholly bad enough to Ufburk, who was presently stretching to get a handhold upwards on the sheer cliff he continued to scale. That a light existed within that shelled creature had been crazy enough, but for it to flick in and out in unison with the one on the Raygun was insanity. Lunacy. Both lights had done what Ufburk recalled, and when the creature had died, and its light extinguished itself. The one on his Raygun stopped cold at that same moment.

The peculiar views had changed from greens to amber and traced patterns around the weapon before resuming that familiar crimson blip. Nothing surrounding the blaster had changed after that; that same crimson button still flashed on and off. In the back of his brain, Ufburk began to believe that those red blips likely meant another monstrosity to face. And that monster would have a red light on its beating heart to put out as well. In union with his belief, the strobe on the Raygun was growing brighter as if he fast approached danger.

This climb would end with a section of rock only the "foolish brave" as Danno called such folk, would dare scale. Ufburk fixed his dry eyes on the slab of granite. He'd soon be suspended in mid-air as he would have to hang underneath that ledge, clinging mostly to rocks, or wishfully, roots if the gods willed. The ridge's stony end pointed outwards, however, and Ufburk thought he could manage to hook his legs around the tip of the jutting rock to get on top of the stone. From there, the climb seemed possible.

After several shaky moments, and through iron-will, Ufburk did pull himself atop the stone. There he squatted to regain his breath before pressing upwards. The empty cavern his lungs left of his chest gasped for oxygen, and spots crawled near the edges of his sight. With his adrenaline faded after the alien threat in his village had passed Ufburk felt hollow somehow. Maybe he was just lonely; he'd sent his pup Sefer back to his cousin's sheep ranch. A dog could not climb cliffsides, and the Barbarian felt grateful for this. Ufburk wanted nothing else for Sefer but for the animal to live a long and natural life. Danno's sheep would keep the pup both happy and busy. Herding sheep even sounded vaguely appealing to Ufburk just then, but he was no fool, adventuring had infected his blood.

Up he went, digging his toes in here, squeezing his knees there while cramming his sore and bleeding fingertips into brutally tight crevices to provide tenuous grips that helped him climb. Up, always and steadily up.

The night went fully black. The low warm breezes from earlier that day had gone stiff and cold. Each time the red light on the Raygun flashed Ufburk used the radiance to gauge his next round of holds and then when the beacon flashed yet again, the Barbarian shifted his ascent upwards. His face burned wildly from the cold wind cutting at his colorless cheeks. Finally, and with much effort, Ufburk reached the peak of the jagged mountaintop he'd spied from Danno's field the day before.

He could see nothing in the gullies below. All was pitch black. Not daring to go into such darkness just yet, Ufburk decided to wait. The stars did twinkle above, but nothing illuminated the canyons below him. It was best to wait. Perhaps things would come clearer with daybreak, but gods knew it would likely be dark on that canyon floor whether he went during the daytime or not.

The thought of waiting until first light agitated him. Still, no other alternative seemed plausible. Going down into those gullies might spell death in the daytime, but evidently the act meant doom in full darkness.

The first few hours under a crescent moon and a bed full of stars crept by slowly, like visitors hesitant to take their leave. At some point, Ufburk heard something wail below and that scream getting cut off suddenly, as if by death. No doubt death lurked below, the hunter in him knew this well enough.

By the looks of the moon, cast lavender in the violet-dark sky night would slide away sufficiently if he could wait it out. The ridge he was on lasted for more than a mile, but for how far he couldn't say. Noting the slope he stood on was reasonably comprehensive and even had grassy meadowlands upon its dark soil, Ufburk surmised he'd reached the summit of an odyssey as mountains went. This mountain was sheer on three sides, and with terrible scaling involved, but the fourth slope, while steep, was fully negotiable.

All this Ufburk saw when pale sunlight began to appear behind him with the coming day.

His thoughts were interrupted by a series of shrieks, surely of a dying polecat, nearer than the last expirations he'd heard. The anguish of those cries found a place within Ufburk that was tender. It hurt to take part in the dying cat's torment, to understand the creature's last. Then, as before, the meadow fell awkwardly silent.

Shaken slightly, Ufburk dusted off his square cut shaggy mane, looking again to the skies. His thoughts no longer lingered on the stars as they had, now he thought only of the cries from below him. What did they mean? But instinctually, Ufburk knew. Something strange and not of his world stalked the lower lands. And it was a hunter-killer, a foul thing from some far-reaching abyss Ufburk could not imagine.

Suddenly Ufburk became aware that a nearby flock of vultures had flown off in haste. Before he had time to register fully what the vultures were frightened by his ears heard a peculiar whirring sound. He'd tried to dive when something pliable but strong netted him. Heavy footsteps trotted up behind Ufburk's back, and he felt something round and cold between his shoulder blades. Then all went ebon.

***

He awoke on a giant plate of cold metal. Groggy as though he was, he felt the netting that had ensnared him, encasing him still. He couldn't flex his muscles any easier than he could move at first, the durable carbon polymer mesh of the bonds had proved themselves a formidable obstacle for the astonished Barbarian.

The ties holding him fast were not the primary source of

117

Ufburk's growing amazement. He lay on the floor of a diamond shaped room, forged of bright silver metal. Embedded in these sloping platinum walls Ufburk's bewildered gaze saw skulls, bleached white and stripped of all flesh. His primitive brain knew at once where he was, even if he had no conception of what, or who but the gods could forge a chamber from metal. It was a trophy room. Ufburk studied the various alcoves, all containing one skull each. Upon further examination, Ufburk saw plainly that no two trophies were the same. Those were the heads of different creatures, and he was in the hunter's trophy room.

As he struggled against his bonds, the Barbarian felt a familiar lump pressed against the side of his left leg, and another pushed against his ribs on his right. That second lump could only be the blaster. Through wriggling, Ufburk managed to angle the Raygun towards the netting and away from himself. After more struggle, the Barbarian was able to depress the trigger. Nothing happened. The weapon was dark. Its fury had gone cold. Even the light strobed no more.

Dismayed, Ufburk attempted to move the ax and found the gods were with him. The bladed edge of Tiber's ax, forged of Verudian Steel cut away the web with considerable ease. Once a hole was established it took the Barbarian scant seconds to gain independence from the net.

The Barbarian was again on his feet. The smooth metal walls about him would have proved folly to any but the best of climbers. The alien trophy room had one entrance that was heavily sealed and an open vent in the ceiling forty feet above him. Ufburk tried the door, and the effort was a wasted one. Nothing could budge that mammoth entrance. No typical climber, and stronger still than many he found his way up and through the vent, where he had to crawl serpentine style inside tight spaces.

118

Leaving the trophy room behind afforded Ufburk's terrified mind a small dose of temporary relief. He heard the same humming now that he'd heard before god's furies wrecked his village. Except he was inside the sound. His skin went damp and cold. Ufburk shuddered at the thought, inside and out.

Moving with grace for such a large man in so tight of space the Barbarian headed towards the opening ahead. Mindful of all noise, his as well as his surroundings, Ufburk peered into the vent hole.

He nearly gasped aloud at the demonic form he saw, back to him, looking through a wall of gleaming glass into a blanket of stars and meteorites. To Ufburk meteorites resembled boulders floating in endless blackness.

Baffled, he remained frozen and thus concealed behind the vaguely humanoid form standing on the ship's observation deck. It did not move, so Ufburk studied the thing carefully. Watching the situation did nothing to ease his surmounting fears. Its back exposed heavy armor like that of an armadillo or tortoise from the dessert lands on Tark.

It wore a chain on an iron-cast collar about its neck and was otherwise sexless and nude. Spiny skin covered its front and legs. The thing had a strange head that looked more like a reptilian fly than men. Reflected in the glass its eyes were like slick marbles covered in pasty goo. Those visual delights sizzled an odd shade of magenta. An inferno of hate hung about the thing. Again Ufburk cringed.

Fate had its way with the Barbarian as he waited in his dusty hidey-hole. His nose began to itch and his eyes watered in streams. He struggled against nature, to maintain his anonymity, but fate is a fickle one. Ufburk sneezed loudly.

Without further warning and already discovered, the Barbarian sprang like a panther from the shadows, landing not three feet from his reeling captor.

The creature's thick skin glowed eerily in the gloomy twilight. Azure tinged its spiky and spotted flesh, and dark grays dominated the creature's thick shell, which virtually covered the thing's back. Such features were demonic enough, but when Ufburk's captor had spun to meet his gaze, the Barbarian shrunk backward, shivering at what he saw. Those inky eyes, sticky-wet and poisonous leered at him from behind a hawk-beaked mouth, set into a pointedly broad jaw with straw shaped incisors capable of perforating his flesh and humungous molars with which to grind him to a pulp.

The Barbarian aimed the Raygun, squeezing the trigger just before the weapon was knocked away by a clawed hand. It had not mattered, the gun did not fire. Out with his ax, Ufburk slashed at the creature. His swipe met with a firm backhand that left Ufburk stumbling to stay upright. From the corner of his wild eyes, widened by shock, Ufburk saw the blaster, its button-light dead, sliding across the floor.

Again and again Ufburk swung at the thing, which moved as swiftly as he could. The beast's malevolent stare shook the young fighter as much as the creature's appearance had. Steeling his resolve, the Barbarian bellowed his war cry. His anger burned red. Actions replaced thought as he dodged and parried the thing's claws. At first glance, Ufburk had thought that this was all they were, claws, the same as a mud crab. When this proved to not be the case, and he saw those hands working almost like his, save for a thumb claw was connect to twin split talons that were as wide as two fingers.

Ufburk let his weapon fly, swinging the ax with all his

considerable might. The creature did not dodge the blow, but rather spun, retracting its head like a tortoise. The Verudian Ax clanged heavily into the bony shell and rang as it was ripped from the Barbarian's grip. The ax spun across the slick metal floor. Ufburk watched it go.

Seizing the opportunity, the creature dashed at the distracted warrior and caught him in around the chest. The creature squeezed mightily. Ufburk felt his left hand going numb, a rib snapped. Pain traced a white lightning rush up his side.

Wriggling, the Barbarian managed to free his right arm. With his right hand, he pried his thumb under the thing's left thumb-claw. His muscles corded and strained with his one mighty effort. Transparent mush oozed from the creature's wound. One backhand from the monster sent the young warrior sailing. The wind left him as he collapsed full-force into the unforgiving floor.

Finally, while his back pressed against that glass wall where stars floated by, Ufburk managed to break his dagger off near the alien's underarm, liquid, sticky and blue seeped from the open wound. The hilt of the weapon clattered to the floor, forgotten. Ufburk's fist crashed into the thing's hawk nose, causing a satisfying crunch under his knuckles.

The thing shrieked, tearing a sizable row into Ufburk's chest with one clawed hand. Instantly the Barbarian struck out at the hand that wounded him.

Diving for the ax, he gained it, and his feet with catlike grace. The Verudian Ax sang a song in the air. Seconds later the creature's wounded hand lie twitching on the floor. The fiend raised its bleeding stump to its eyes. Ufburk's ax fell once more, cleaving through the alien's collarbone and chest plating. Recoiling the Demoki Demon fell half backward to its knees. Malice raged in the creature's strange eyes.

Impaired, the creature crawled at Ufburk as he retrieved his blaster from the observatory floor. The weapon did not fire, but rather lit again with an amber light, the eerie pattern traced the gun's outline once more. Three flashes of emerald light lit the button, as Ufburk swung the ax left-handed, striking the beast's collarbone and opening its breastbone wide.

The blinking crimson light on the Raygun appeared, pulsing and as strong as before. There, between split bone and cartilage, bathing in a lake of bluish-black blood, Ufburk saw the heart of his enemy. Incredibly from within that heart strobed a crimson beacon. The Barbarian placed the muzzle of the gun against his fallen enemy's slow-throbbing heart. Before he could fire a spike shot from the under weapon's muzzle, impaling the creature's heart and stopping it cold.

Ufburk watched again in fascination as the red lights blinked out and the gun went dead and stared helplessly out the glass at the starry sky he floated in through some wicked sorcery or another. He stood there for some time, a Barbarian staring dumbly at the stars. They were a wonderment, and Ufburk supposed this was probably all anybody really knew about the stars. Picking up the Raygun, he set off to explore the craft. No others were aboard. When he came to a paneled cockpit, full of dazzlingly lighted displays, all those dancing lights went out. Again he peered into starry space.

What will I do?

That singular thought must have woken the powers, because now, upon the dash panel a lava red beacon sprung to life and on the Raygun, cold until then, the same. They beat in tandem. Ufburk heard a new hum strike up, and the vessel began to move. Bewildered, the Barbarian sunk into the seat nearest him while shaking his head in disgust, and knowing dark days lie ahead for him. So on that day, Ufburk left his homeworld of Tark behind.

What followed after is another story.

The End

The Serpent Bearer and the Prince of Stars
By C. S. Johnson

The heavens were alight with festive fire and a cheering crowd. Many had arrived to the Kingdom Hall's celebration singing, overflowing with happiness and joy, and others were still pouring in as he watched. Friends easily came together, radiating smiles and bouncing back laughter as they talked, joked, and prattled on with each other. He could hear several discussing the beauty and majesty all around, and he had to admit they were right to do so; no measure had been spared in making the party grand, unusual as it was for such festivity to be had. Or at least, unusual for him. It wasn't like he was invited to parties very often. No one cared about him.

No one cared about him, and they had not cared for some time, Ophiuchus thought with a grimace as he backed into a nearby corner. It was going to be a long and lonely night, where he would face constant reminders of his disconnected existence from the other stars, angels, and constellations who had come to the great hall.

"You're not alone." The voice from behind his ear

almost surprised him; in concentrating on his impending night of being ostracized, he'd momentarily forgotten the reason for it. Ophiuchus turned to see the slanted, gleaming eyes of his ward–the snake he'd been charged with keeping. "I'm here."

"If coming means arriving with you, I would have rather stayed behind," Ophiuchus grumbled. "Why did you have to come tonight, Naga?"

"You know as well as I do that I go where you go," the snake hissed. As if to remind Ophiuchus of the most painful aspect of that fact, Naga constricted his long, scaly body more tightly around Ophiuchus' neck, hands, and feet.

Ophiuchus, after all the time Naga had been assigned to him, was used to the pain. "I would have thought the Kingdom Hall would have been enough to send you away."

Naga's face contorted in something of a smile. "Even I know you don't believe that, or you would not have come; the other invitations from your former friends and associates of the Zodiac have gone ignored. We are only here, both of us, because it was the Prince who invited us."

That was true, Ophiuchus admitted to himself. He sighed and felt Naga's body tighten around him once more, as though he sensed he'd won the argument.

"I would have thought the Prince would have refrained from inviting you," the snake whispered with a smug look. "Maybe he invited you by mistake."

Ophiuchus again said nothing. He had spent centuries upon centuries arguing with Naga, and he was getting more and more tired of it, and at the serpent's assertion, Ophiuchus felt the weight of all the years eat away at him.

Before Naga could take another swipe at him, Ophiuchus heard someone call out to him.

"Ophiuchus! Ophiuchus, over here." The clatter of a ram's hooves grew louder as Aries, one of his Zodiac brothers, approached him. There was a telling smile on his face which made Ophiuchus groan.

"Come on, Aries, I don't want to have a match," Ophiuchus muttered. "And neither does Naga. It is one of the few things on which we agree."

"Speak for yourself," Naga countered. "I'd love the opportunity to snap at Aries' silly snout."

Aries bucked. "Keep your fangs to yourself, viper."

"I'm not a viper," the serpent cooed. "I didn't know rams were so bad at seeing things. Too many hits to the head, perhaps?"

"Aries has always been curious," Ophiuchus insisted, reaching up and squeezing the jaws of his charge shut. He wasn't able to completely avoid the resulting bite, but he'd grown immune to Naga's venom.

Aries stood on his hind legs, drawing himself to his full height. "That's right," he asserted. "And you'd do well to remember that, snake." He turned his full attention back to Ophiuchus, who only looked resigned. "That does remind me, though, Ophiuchus, why are you here? Surely this is not something you would do without some kind of compulsion."

"The Prince invited me," Ophiuchus explained. "So I came."

"Are you sure?" Aries asked. "I haven't seen him yet."

"It's not often Kingdom Hall calls together all the stars and angels for a celebration," Ophiuchus said.

"Considering the amount of people here, I'd say he was very intentional about having the party."

"I wasn't talking about that," Aries corrected him. "I was talking about whether the Prince meant to invite you or not."

"You'll have to excuse Ophiuchus," Naga spoke up. "He just thinks you're overbearing and stupid, so he had to make sure he clarified the obvious."

"What? Naga, that's—" Ophiuchus sighed as Aries huffed and turned away. "You shouldn't have said that, Naga. Aries is a nice guy."

"Nice guys are more than capable of being stupid," Naga snapped. "Just look at you. You're supposed to be so nice, and when the Prince of Stars hands me to you, you just took me." His eyes narrowed with malicious hatred. "Stupid."

Ophiuchus suddenly wondered if Naga had a point. He remembered when the Prince had come to him, all those long years ago, asking for Ophiuchus to help him. Ophiuchus, one of the lesser Zodiac siblings, had been eager—perhaps too eager—for the opportunity to assist his ruler. The Prince had been sad that day; there was an expression on his brightly glowing face, and a new depth to the fiery crystals of his eyes. That alone had made Ophiuchus, who loved the Prince, want to do anything to please him and to make him happy once more.

"I might have been stupid in taking you," Ophiuchus agreed, "but I would have been even more stupid to say no to the Prince of Stars."

"You've talked to the Prince of Stars, Ophiuchus?" A high-pitched laugh followed the inquiry, as Taurus passed by. "I'm surprised you would tell such a story.

It's not like you to assert your claim to fame; at least, it hasn't been, since you've gotten that serpent." Taurus flicked her long tail playfully over her shoulder as she looked at him with pity. "Which I see you still have."

Naga hissed in appreciation, and Ophiuchus was sure the snake caught the derision in her tone same as he had. Ophiuchus gave his best smile back. "Naga is under my care until the Prince wants him back."

"I'm sure," Taurus muttered dismissively. "It doesn't seem like the Prince is the kind of person to give one a duty as demanding and cruel as this one. After all, he's only asked me to help with the Zodiac duties once every year on Earth. You really ought to think about getting rid of Naga on your own. That is," she added, "if you are not so attached to him."

"Ophiuchus and I are pretty close," Naga said with a smirk. "Right, Ophiuchus?" He once more squeezed his body around Ophiuchus' neck.

Ophiuchus quickly responded in kind, grabbing Naga just under his devilish grin. Naga released his grip, but Ophiuchus held on, until Taurus, too eager to see her other friends, disappeared as quickly as she'd come.

"I can help you if you need something pinched," a small voice spoke up from the floor.

"Hi, Cancer. I didn't see you down there," Ophiuchus greeted. "I've got a good hold on Naga; please do not worry for me."

The crablike figure, a great deal smaller than his Zodiac brothers, carefully reached out one of his claws. "I haven't seen you at recent functions, Ophiuchus, and you used to be so cheerful and loud. Your voice was strong, and you looked forward to challenges. I do worry for you and wish you could get better."

Ophiuchus thought of how nice it would be to get rid of Naga's hold on him. "It's complicated," Ophiuchus murmured. He remembered how sympathetic Cancer had been to him when he'd agreed to keep charge of Naga. Ever since then, he remembered, it was hard to get Cancer to talk of anything but his 'getting better.'

"I just want to see you happy," Cancer remarked, as if he'd read Ophiuchus' mind. "You always seem so lonely and sad now. It's almost like you've given up on being happy or having something worth having."

Ophiuchus smiled. "I have the same as you—a duty to our Prince. Your concern is misplaced, friend."

Cancer shook his head. "I'm not so sure," he said. "I think you're lying to yourself. You need to get over this complex of yours, Ophiuchus. You're only hurting yourself and the people you care about by clinging to it." He scuttled away before Ophiuchus could argue the matter.

"He seems nice." Naga laughed. "He was the one who used to come and visit us, didn't he?"

"Yes." Ophiuchus nodded.

"He was the one who would listen to you talk about me and try to help by telling you he felt sorry for you." Naga laughed harder. "What a joke. He's not a real friend to you."

"You're not either," Ophiuchus reminded him.

"Of course not," Naga agreed. "But you need me now, whether you like it or not. If I'm not around, there's no hope any of the other Zodiac or stars or angels would even pay attention to you. Although," he said, nodding to the crowd, "it's hard to say if they even do that anymore."

"Some have," Ophiuchus argued. "And look, here

comes Sagittarius and Capricorn."

Capricorn, with her fish tail and tiny goat horns, seemed amused to see him. She elbowed Sagittarius. "Look, its Ophiuchus and his snakeskin scarf. I don't really think it goes well with his coloring."

Sagittarius shook her head. "Well, life isn't fair, is it? Sometimes we just need to get over it. Don't we, Ophiuchus?"

"Hello, Sagittarius. Hello, Capricorn." Ophiuchus nodded respectfully to the two of his Zodiac sisters he knew had the most trouble with him.

Capricorn bleated. "Well, don't sound so upset to see me, Ophiuchus. What do you have to be depressed about to begin with?"

"You should be grateful and happy you've even been invited to the party," Sagittarius added.

"You know well Naga and I have been fighting for eons now," Ophiuchus tried to explain. "And sometimes–"

"I offered to take care of him with my bow," Sagittarius interrupted. "You said no, and said no quite a few times." She shrugged. "You can't complain about it if you're not willing to accept help."

"The Prince asked me to watch him," Ophiuchus snapped. "So I'll watch him, no matter what you two say."

"The Prince was probably testing you, to see if your pride would cave before he has to correct you," Capricorn snarled, unhappy Ophiuchus had lashed out. "It was probably a punishment, since you were so insistent that we keep you in the Zodiac family."

"Yes, I don't recall Cetan giving us so much trouble when we talked about making it a band of twelve,"

131

Sagittarius agreed.

"He was fine with being excluded. Of course, he's much happier and much more upbeat than you are. In fact, I was fine with keeping him in the Zodiac. Probably because he didn't try to cut into my time."

Capricorn was definitely ambitious, Ophiuchus knew. She had not been pleased at his intent to stay in the Zodiac constellation, especially after she had pleaded with the Prince himself over the matter. "I know you like watching over Earth, Capricorn," Ophiuchus said. "But there was nothing wrong about wanting to be a part of the family, like I rightfully am. And Cetan has the same privilege as I do. Even if we are not as powerful nor as central to Polaris as you."

"You're just trying to make me feel sorry for you." Capricorn shook her head. "So I'll forgive you for cutting in on my space. But it won't work. Even that snake can't make me feel sorry for you, and I'm even less inclined to sympathize since you've been adamant that the Prince is the one who put him with you."

Two identical figures appeared on the scene. "Capricorn, you really need to let it go," the first one said.

"Yeah, Ophiuchus is not responsible for his pain," the other said. "So you should ignore it. If he wants to say the Prince put him in charge of that hellish creature, let him."

"He's suffering," the other continued. "If saying the Prince put him up to it is something that's going to make him feel better, let him."

Naga laughed. "How do you know I didn't just convince him to keep me? And now that I've got him, I'm never going to let go?" he asked the twins.

Castor, the one on the right, blankly stared at him. Then he blinked, and said, "Ophiuchus was among the strongest in the night skies," he said. "He would have been able to defeat you, if he chose to do so."

Ophiuchus felt the heat rise in his cheeks, angry and frustrated at so many things all at once. He thought about trying to explain everything, all over again, but a couple of other Stars caught his attention. They were laughing and pointing at him from across the hall.

The other twin, Pollux, spoke up before Ophiuchus could excuse himself. "You were brought here from the earth, snake, while Ophiuchus was born of the night. Why would we assume you are stronger than Ophiuchus?"

"I might have come from Earth, but I have death in me," Naga said smoothly. "Even you are not immune to death." He unwrapped himself from Ophiuchus' hands and wrists before rewrapping his body down the length of Ophiuchus' body.

The twins exchanged looks and then, quietly and respectfully, excused themselves. "We wish you the best, Ophiuchus!" they called out, as they stepped back into the glittering celebration. "Good luck in getting better."

Ophiuchus felt defeat sink into his very being. "Let's go," he said to Naga.

"Ooh, but the party has only just begun," Naga said cheerfully, clearing relishing the discordance between Ophiuchus and the others.

"I don't care," Ophiuchus told him. "I'd been asked to come by the Prince, and that's what I did. He didn't tell me how long to stay here, and I'll do as I please for once. That might even help; many here think I am incapable of doing that when it comes to keeping you in line. It will be good of me to show them I am still strong and still capable of choosing to do what makes me happy."

"Good for you," Naga muttered disdainfully. "Take a stand for yourself. I mean, really, after all this time, the Prince has just left me with you, and didn't tell you anything about how long it would be, or even really why he gave me to you. You just can't trust someone who hides the truth of these sorts of things."

"I didn't say that," Ophiuchus murmured. He felt his tongue go dry at the thought of Capricorn's words. Could Naga have been a punishment? "I've been a good servant to my master, and I will continue to do what is right."

"Even when I've done my very worst to keep you unhappy?" Naga chortled with laughter. "I'm honored, I really am. This is perfect! A willing victim is always the best kind of victim."

"I'm not a victim," Ophiuchus countered. "I chose to watch over you."

Naga laughed harder, his snake tongue lashing out of his mouth. "Hilarious!" he hissed. "Not just a victim of his prince, but of his own reasoning, too. See? It is as I told you earlier. You're stupid." Naga shifted his face closer to Ophiuchus. "And you're unhappy, and suffering, and ignored by all your so-called friends, and your so-called brethren of the Zodiac. Even the ones who offered to help you out at first, and even the ones who have only been wishing for you to be rid of me."

Ophiuchus bristled. "I can take care of you, Naga, and I have done so for millennia."

"You're weak, and I only grow stronger as you fade,"

Naga insisted. "We have equal power, but not equal purpose. I just have to wear you down, and make you give up; you can hate me or love me or just tolerate me, but you'll never be able to get me to stop fighting you. It is just as I told the others: Death resides in me, and all of life is just an attempt to keep death at bay. And you will not succeed. Even if I go out along with you, I will have the final victory in the end."

Ophiuchus stopped and felt the full weight and meaning of Naga's words. He almost shuttered, as he realized Naga had solid arguments against him. It was possible Naga would leave him to death, that Naga would destroy his light and his life. "You might one day find such an ending," Ophiuchus said, "but not this day." He reached out and snapped Naga's jaw, catching his sliced tongue between his lips. "Come. We are leaving and heading back to our home. No matter what the party is for, we are not welcome here anymore."

Naga rolled his yellow-green eyes. "You know, you might want to consider a truce between us," he said, his voice silky smooth. He curled his body around Ophiuchus' body, almost like a warm hug, as they stepped out of the Kingdom Hall.

"Why's that?" Ophiuchus asked.

"Because, like it or not, we are unwelcome," Naga said. "You were not welcome even before I came along. You were too busy trying to cut in line between Sags and Capri. They had reason to distrust you and hate you, and with me along, their condemnation is all the more justified in their own minds."

Ophiuchus said nothing as Naga continued.

"Ophiuchus, we could make a very good partnership," Naga insisted. "I can't disobey the Prince of Stars any more than you could–he rules over the earth as easily as he does the Stars and angels–but there's no need for us to be fighting the whole time we're put together, right? Can't you think of some things we've agreed on in the past?"

"No. You always go against me," Ophiuchus remarked.

"Well, you're doing that just now," Naga pointed out. When Ophiuchus did not respond, the snake cackled. "Just think about it. We don't have to be enemies, here, do we? That's the only reason I am making your life hard, isn't it? Because you're letting me, and because you think I'm the enemy. The Prince never said anything about that."

Again, Ophiuchus did not answer.

He thought it over. Naga, as much as he hated to admit it, had a point. He didn't have to make him an enemy. The Prince was the one who saw Naga as dangerous, as a problem. Ophiuchus could probably get along well with Naga. After all the time they'd been together, it was similar to what he suspected a human felt about his shadow; it was a quiet, dark kind of comfortable familiarity, and it was not desirable, perhaps, but it was there, and there was no getting rid of it.

He thought of all his friends who had watched him suffer with Naga suffocating him, and the pain – oh, the memories of the pain had been the worst. Memories of Naga squeezing him, sniping at him, hissing at him, all while the earth kept going around its sun, and the other Zodiac either ignored him or eventually left him to suffer, unable or unwilling to argue with him or deal with him.

136

It was only as they came upon Ophiuchus' home—a bright and shining palace, made of the purest transparent gold, that his thoughts were overtaken.

Ophiuchus was surprised to see the Prince of Stars waiting for him on his doorstep. "Lord? What are you doing here?" he asked.

"What am I doing here?" The Prince smiled kindly. "Shouldn't the question be, 'what are you doing here?' I invited you to come to my party."

"I was just there," Ophiuchus insisted. "I did not disobey you."

"No, you did not," the Prince agreed. "But it is early. The party is not over."

"I thought it best to leave." Ophiuchus could hear the echoes of discouragement, judgment, and alienation. He looked up into the Prince's eyes without holding back.

"Such sorrow." The Prince shook his head. "It is never easy, bearing a burden. And it is harder yet to bear one which no one understands."

Ophiuchus stepped back. "I chose this," he said. "I understand it is much harder than I thought it would be. I didn't realize just what you were asking of me. I don't think I am the right one to look after Naga anymore." He looked at the snake, who had gone silent in the Prince's presence. "I'm not strong enough to carry on for much longer, and I just want to be happy again, and to have the respect of the others. Please, my lord, please take this pain from me, and forgive me for being so weak."

"You've carried this for so long. You are stronger than you realize," he said. "There is no need for apology." The Prince then looked at him. "Ophiuchus, do you know the reason I invited you to the party tonight?"

"No, lord."

"Tonight is a special night; tonight, one of my promises is going to be fulfilled. I have need for Naga," he said. "I am going to release him back down to Earth, because the time has come for his head to be crushed by the heel he tried to poison."

"He will be punished?" Ophiuchus asked. Naga, still silent, fell limp around his body.

"Do you think it is wrong to punish him?" asked the Prince.

Naga lay across his arms, still alive and warm. Ophiuchus felt all the burden of all the long years retreat, and the spirit inside of him grew. His muscles were taut, and his body, now completely upright, and he felt all his world within him and around him swell with happiness and goodness. Ophiuchus looked back at the Prince. "For a while, I thought he would be nothing but trouble," he said. "I thought I was doing something for you to show you I could be of help to you. But I know from Naga I am not able to help you as much as I'd like, that I'm not needed for your work to get done. I think of all the things he has put me through, and all the things I have been through as a result. He tried to call himself my friend, but he is no one's friend. He has done nothing but try to dissuade me from following you. He brings nothing but division between me and my friends and family. He is my enemy." Ophiuchus blinked, as though hearing it for the first time from his own words made it more real and clearer than ever before. "He is my enemy."

"So what is your answer?" the Prince asked.

A moment passed between them before Ophiuchus spoke again. "Your will should be done," Ophiuchus answered. "He has brought both good and bad into my life; you will judge him according to what is right."

The Prince of Stars reached out and took hold of Ophiuchus. "Let's go back to the party and give him a proper send off."

Ophiuchus smiled as Naga, his mouth still sealed shut, could only scowl. All of his trouble, all of Ophiuchus' pain and longsuffering, all of it suddenly seemed worth it, to get to this moment.

The End

Chaos on Cass
By Chris Raven

Part Four: Confrontation

Cass III (The Third Planet of the Eta Cassiopeiae System, 20LY from Sol and held in fealty for the Terran Star Empire by the Imperial House of Lein Rocha)

The Watcher

The Interrogator is getting close now. He knows the identities of those that were in the cell, the cell he has single handily decimated. He currently turns his attention towards me, following his victims' trail back to their leader. I am strangely exhilarated, no one has come this close before. I am only one step ahead of him, the efficacy of a single person's psychological inhibitor is all that stands between my hunter and me. I wonder if that person will withstand The Interrogator's skilled and persistent probing. I wonder also if The Telepath will remain loyal to his home or finally completely join the regime that suppresses his people. Ah! Here they come now, I suspect I am about to find out.

Now!

"Thank you for seeing me again Captain Beydo." Sam approached the large puffy faced Chief of Police, who scowled at him from behind his desk. Ignoring Sam's outstretched hand again as he motioned him to sit down opposite.

"You killed the Governor's Secretary's daughter," this was a statement of fact, not a question.

"And you had your informant killed, sorry, I mean executed." Beydo shrugged.

"Him? Higani here can tell you all about him, can't you Vasco." Higani, from his position just behind Sam's right shoulder, shifted his feet uncomfortably under his superior's gaze.

"He already has," Sam advised the chief of police, who leant forward, eyeing from across the desk with undisguised contempt.

"Then you know he was a paid informant, an asset I had hoped would get us close to what we suspected was a dangerous nest of dissidents."

"Yet you had him killed," Sam reminded him.

"He was no good to me anymore was he," Beydo accused, slamming a hand down loudly with a sharp slap, "not after you'd finished with 'im."

This was not going as well as Sam had hoped. It seemed that Beydo was going to try and bluff it out, so Sam decided to take a direct approach.

"Did you recruit Melissa Guzman, Paccoro Otero and Jorge Alvero into a secret terrorist organisation?" Beydo stared at Sam in disbelief for a few seconds before bursting out into a deep rolling laugh.

"My god man," he spluttered, "are you mad?"

The standoff lasted an hour, Beydo stanchly

maintaining that he had been leading a covert operation, running Alvero as a double agent. Sam on the other had damn well knew that he was lying, but could not challenge directly without revealing himself to be an Empath. It was Higani who finally broke the stalemate.

"Chief," he suddenly interrupted," please sir, give it up." Sam and Beydo stopped what had become a pointless circular argument and Sam craned his head round to see what the usually reticent lieutenant had to say

"Vasco?" Sam sensed hurt surprise from Beydo.

"Chief," Higani continued, his voice quiet and regretful, "Harford please, you know you can't lie to me, I see your confession as clear as if you had written it on a datapad."

As Sam turned back to confront the Chief he sensed a sudden change in his mood, a mixture of anger, fear and resolve. By the time he had turned to face Beydo, the Chief was already aiming a laser pistol at him. An impulsive move on Beydo's part, otherwise Sam would have been ready for him.

The Watcher

Now I know. The Telepath has shown his true colours and has sided with The Interrogator. Interesting that a native Cassian would side with the regime while a Lein Rochan executive remains loyal to the cause. I had such hope for Higani, his abilities would have been useful in the rebellion, the cause to bring House Lein Rocha down to its knees. It has taken me a long time to get where I am now, to a position of influence and power. I will not let it end here, now, like this.

143

Now!

"Now Beydo," Sam said cautiously, holding his hand up open palmed, "let's not do anything rash, there's still a way out of this for you, but not if you kill me."

"Shut up you scrawny little bastard," Beydo snapped, "You know as well as I do the only outcome for me is a firing squad." With sharp angry gestures, Beydo told Sam and Higani to keep their hands in view, Higani with his held up like some sap from an old pulp crime vid and Sam, palms down on the desk top before him. Sam could sense Higani's inner conflict, he was torn between loyalty to his office and loyalty to his friend. There was also fear, which told Sam that Beydo was capable of anything. Beydo on the other hand had become calm, resolved even, a state of mind which scared Sam the most as it made Beydo unpredictable.

"So what happens now? Sam asked.

"What do you suggest," Beydo sneered, "a soliloquy? Is this where I describe my devious plot before surrendering gracefully?" Sam forced a smile, trying to appear relaxed, trying to encourage some empathy from the man on the other side of the table. The man with the gun, the man who had hated him from the moment they had met.

"No," Sam agreed, "I won't insult you, you're perfectly correct. Eventually we will kill you. You are Lein Rochan, you know it is the only way. Your only chance is to barter for how and when it happens. Tell me the identity of any remaining dissidents in your organisation, provide us with a full account of your operation and I will personally ensure that your final days are very comfortable and you have a painless death at the end of it."

"Huh!" Beydo snorted.

"It's your only chance Harford," Higani interrupted. Beydo gave him a cold stare before turning his attention back to Sam.

"Alright," he said finally, after contemplating the specialist agent's dark eyes for a few seconds, "I'll cooperate, I'll tell you what you want to know. I'm the last, there is no one left under me, you have killed them all."

"Higani!" Sam asked and the telepath confirmed that Beydo was telling the truth.

"Beydo," Sam continued, "I need you to put down the gun before we can discuss any terms regarding your arrest and subsequent treatment." Beydo just stared back expressionlessly and then he smiled.

"Harford No!" That was Higani screaming from behind Sam, just seconds before Beydo turned his laser on himself and disintegrated a sizable portion of his head.

The Watcher

I am safe, Beydo's conditioning held out and his loyalty led him to the only action he had left. A cell is destroyed and a potential recruit is lost, though I may not give up on The Telepath just yet, he would make an invaluable asset, if only I could find a lever. The Interrogator? He is satisfied and will leave this planet to report that all is now well here on Cass.

Yes, it is a shame, years of planning wasted, Beydo's cell, central to my plot, now gone, delaying everything by years. But overall? It is merely a delay, the inevitable will go ahead and I am a very patient man.

I will now remotely short-circuit the surveillance devices in Beydo's office, long before they can be discovered and tracked back to me. There, I am safe again, all links to Beydo now severed.

I have already activated one of my other cells, a member of which is visiting my employer this very moment. Ah! My employer calls.

"One moment Sir," I tell him via the intercom, "I shall be along directly."

I am Jaikab again, the loyal servant to a bereaved government official. The interview is over and I am to show his guest out of the mansion. I have made sure that she is the best of all the available candidates, ideal for the post of personal assistant, someone who can assist my poor employer in keeping ahead of his duties during this difficult time. Maybe she will become an invaluable aide, a friend and confident, maybe even a surrogate daughter to replace the one he lost. Either that or maybe a lover in time. For now however, she only needs to take away some of the burden while he organises his daughter's funeral.

The End.

ABOUT THE AUTHORS

Chris Raven

Chris Raven was born in South London just shy of 50 years ago. He originally started out in Theatre in the 1980s but he became side-tracked by health and social care, where he has made his living for the past 25 or so years. More recently he has found his way back to the creative arts by contributing a number of short stories to the Indie Collaboration's series of free anthologies.

He has also contributed illustrations to other author's works and has been coordinating a shared writing project with other new writers called 'Tall Stories'. A relative newcomer to fiction, he is currently experimenting with a number of different formats and genres, including poetry, short storytelling and playwriting.

Find Chris at **www.chrisravenblog.wordpress.com**

Regina Puckett

Regina Puckett is a 2014 Readers' Favorite Award winning author for her sweet romance, *Concealed in My Heart*. Her steampunk book, *I Will Breathe*, and her children's picture book, *Borrowed Wings*, both received the Children's Literary Classic Seal of Approval.

I Will Breathe is a 2015 winner in the science fiction category in the Readers' Favorite Book Awards and was a finalist in the IAN Book Awards. *Memories*, won first place in the 1st WSBR International Poetry Contest, and her collection of poetry, Fireflies, won the 2013 Turning Pages Poetry Book of the Year.

She writes sweet romances, horror, inspirational, steampunk, picture books and poetry. There are always several projects in various stages of completion and characters and stories waiting in the wings for their chance to finally get out of her head and onto paper.

Please come and visit me at facebook.com/regina.puckett1

http://reginapuckettsbooks.weebly.com/index.html

http://www.goodreads.com/author/show/154116.Regina_ Puckett

https://twitter.com/ReginaPucket

Also by Regina Puckett:

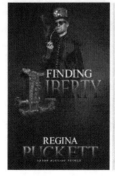 

Dani J Caile

After a lifetime of reading clones and a decade of proofreading coffee table books, Dani J Caile began writing in 2011 and has written many books, including 'Man by a tree', 'The Bethlehem Fiasco', 'The Rage of Atlantis', the infamous 'Manna-X' and his latest 'How to Build a Castle in Seven Easy Steps', published by Line by Lion Publications.

He has also self-published many short story compilations on Smashwords.com called 'Dani's Shorts' available for free and based on the 500 word weekly Iron Writer Challenge, and some of his work can be found in other anthologies, such as 'Circuits & Steam', and publications from the Indie Collaboration. When not writing, teaching English and proofreading, he is busy with his loving and long-suffering family.

http://danijcaile.blogspot.in

Also by Dani J Caile

Peter John

Peter John was born in Bromley Kent, England in 1973. He gained an interest in creative writing at the age of 14 and was published during the 1990s in several poetry anthologies.

Happily Married to Jo since 1996 and currently living in Sidcup Kent, not so far from the tree.

Also by Peter John

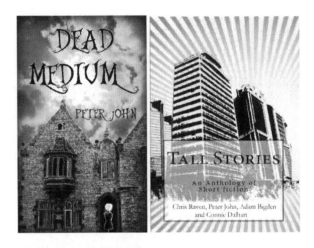

Kalyan Mattaparthi

Madhu Kalyan Mattaparthi is an IT professional from Hyderabad, India, born on 16th January 1989. He is a philanthropist, traveller and pursues writing as a hobby. Sensitive and observant, everything that happens around him is an inspiration to do something new. His knowledge in the world of technology has earned him appreciation and success and he now considers writing his new passion. He has worked in Google, India as a CEA and also the owner of a start-up company, Green Turtle Software Solutions.

Previously Published in:

James Gordon

James Gordon (also known as G.P.A. or The Greatest Poet Alive) is from Chicago Illinois and is the author of the Amazon Best Seller "Hi My Name is Bobo"(A Weekend in the Life of a 5th Grader).

He is the winner of the Moth Storytelling Slam, Poetry Pentathlon, and Black Essence Award, as well as having been nominate Poet of the Year for three years and Book of the Year twice.

Also by James Gordon

Donny Swords

Donny Swords is no stranger to the Indie Collaboration and is pleased to be back for another round. Ufburk is pleased as well.

C. S. Johnson

C. S. Johnson is the author of The Starlight Chronicles series for young adults. With a gift of sarcasm and an apologetic heart, she currently lives in Atlanta with her family, cats, and caffeine addiction. Follow her on Twitter @C_S_Johnson13.

Ray Foster

Whatever I write has a soundtrack – in this case Amaranthe's 'The Nexus' and Delain's 'We Are The Others'. The video game in this story 'Titanfall' exists and I play it. The story grew from a thousand word piece that I wrote during my time with the Felixstowe Scribblers. However, I do wonder what happened next – so, maybe, it will grow some more.

OTHER PUBLICATIONS BY
THE INDIE COLLABORATION

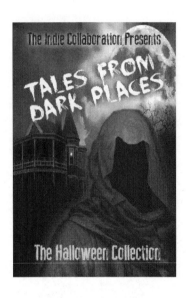

**TALES FROM DARK PLACES: THE
HALLOWEEN COLLECTION**

A selection of chilling stories from some of the best
indie authors on the market. We dare you to
venture into these pages of spine chilling tales and
stories of ghosts and goblins. Freely donated by the
authors themselves, these dark passages are a great
example of their various, unique styles and
imaginations. This is the first of a series of free
topical collections brought to you by The Indie
Collaboration.

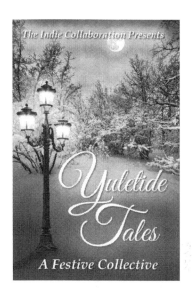

YULETIDE TALES: A FESTIVE COLLECTIVE

A diverse collection of stories showcasing some of the best indie authors on the market. Filled with heart-warming romance, mysterious humour, sinister, supernatural thrills and tearful sorrow, this anthology has something for everyone. So snuggle up with a warm glass of mulled wine and join us for the festivities, while we lift your spirit, tickle your fancy and rattle your bones.

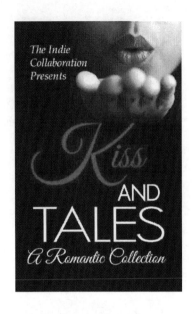

**KISS AND TALES: A ROMANTIC
COLLECTION**

Another collection of free original tales brought to
you by The Indie Collaboration. This time we
present a chocolate box selection of love stories.
Some are romantic, some funny, some sad and
some mysterious. Whatever the style, there will be
a story in here that will melt even the most
hardened of hearts.

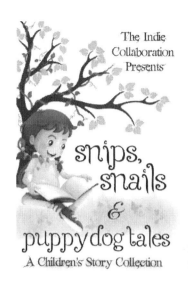

The Indie
Collaboration
Presents

snips,
snails
&
puppydog tales
A Children's Story Collection

**SNIPS, SNAILS & PUPPY DOG TALES: A
CHILDREN'S STORY COLLECTION**

Another collection of free poems and stories
brought to you by The Indie Collaboration. This
time we take you to a world of dreams. To far-
away lands of magic and wonder, where ducks and
children have adventures and learn about the
world; where heroes help their friends and
elephants get lost.

So pack your lunch box, grab your coat and shoes
and join us in a land of make believe.
I can't wait. Can you?

SUMMER SHORTS
An eclectic collection of stories from various
authors. From action filled Science Fiction to dark
sinister chills, humorous mystery, and wild impish
fun.

Ideal for relaxing in the summer sun.

SPECTACULAR TALES
A thrilling anthology of short stories by some of the rising stars in independent publishing. In this collection we bring you a ship's locker full of great Science Fiction and Fantasy. There are tales about beautiful princesses and cunning thieves, intergalactic wars, cosmic energy beings, warriors and rocketship pilots.

So strap on your jet pack and grab your broadsword and come join us in exploring these 'Spectacular Tales'.

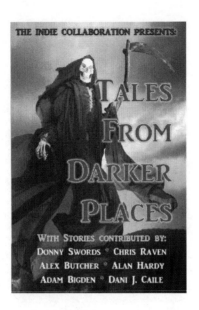

TALES FROM DARKER PLACES

A selection of chilling stories from some of the best Indie authors on the market. We dare you to venture into these pages of spine chilling tales and stories of dark shadows & darker tidings, shifters, ancient warriors, zombies, & demons… See the world through the Ripper's eyes, and so much more. So many dark, foul things wait for you between these pages. Freely donated by the authors themselves, these dark passages are a great example of their various, unique styles and imaginations.

Join us in Darker Places.

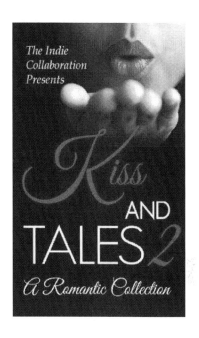

The Indie
Collaboration
Presents

Kiss

AND

TALES 2

A Romantic Collection

KISS and TALES 2

In 2014, The Indie Collaboration was happy to offer
a diverse collection of free short stories and
romantic poetry highlighting a wonderful group of
authors from all over the world. This year they're
back with a new collection of romance and poetry
for you to enjoy on Valentine's Day.

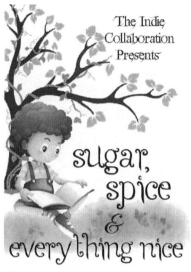

The Indie
Collaboration
Presents

sugar,
spice
&
everything nice

A Second Collection of Children's Stories

Sugar, Spice and Everything Nice
Another collection of children's stories and poems
from The Indie Collaboration. Once again we take
you to far-away lands of magic and moonbeams,
wishes and daydreams, cookies and ice creams.

I can't wait to go back. Can you?

Made in the USA
Lexington, KY
14 March 2017